'I guess it's because I'm nervous.'

'Nervous?' he repeated.

'It's so silly,' she blurted out. 'It's not as though I'm a virgin.'

'Maybe not,' he said, his eyes soft on her. 'But it will be your first time in a long time. And your first time with me.'

'Yes,' she whispered through parched lips.

When Sebastian took hold of her hand, an electric current raced up her arm. Apprehension gave way to anticipation, and doubt was replaced by the most overwhelming need—not to be made love to, but to be totally ravaged. Her head turned and her eyes locked with his.

'Don't be gentle with me,' she heard herself say.

He stared at her for a long moment, then nodded. 'Your wish is my command.'

Miranda Lee is Australian, living near Sydney. Born and raised in the bush, she was boarding-school educated and briefly pursued a career in classical music, before moving to Sydney and embracing the world of computers. Happily married, with three daughters, she began writing when family commitments kept her at home. She likes to create stories that are believable, modern, fast-paced and sexy. Her interests include meaty sagas, doing word puzzles, gambling and going to the movies.

Recent titles by the same author:

PLEASURED IN THE BILLIONAIRE'S BED
LOVE-SLAVE TO THE SHEIKH

THE RUTHLESS MARRIAGE PROPOSAL

BY
MIRANDA LEE

First published in Great Britain 2007
Harlequin Mills & Boon Limited,
Eton House, 18-24 Paradise Road, Richmond, Surrey TW9 1SR

© Miranda Lee 2007

ISBN-13: 978 0 263 19604 7
ISBN-10:   0 263 19604 6

Set in Times Roman
07-0407-39980

Printed and bound in Great Britain
by Antony Rowe Ltd, Chippenham, Wiltshire

THE RUTHLESS MARRIAGE PROPOSAL

CHAPTER ONE

*Sydney airport. Eight o'clock. One Friday
evening in March.*

'THANK YOU for flying with us, Mr Armstrong,' the
female flight attendant purred as Sebastian disem-
barked through the first class exit.

He nodded and hurried on by, anxious to get out
to the taxi rank before the hordes descended.
Thankfully, he'd only brought a cabin bag with him
and didn't have to collect any luggage.

The warm air outside the air-conditioned terminal
came as a shock and Sebastian was glad to step into
a taxi with minimal delay. He momentarily thought
of ringing Emily to let her know he'd caught an
earlier flight, but decided against it. It wasn't as
though he needed her to cook him dinner, and really,
he wasn't in the mood to talk.

All he wanted was to get home…

* * *

Emily's hands trembled as she picked up her resignation letter from the computer printer and read it through.

Just a few simple sentences, yet it had taken her over an hour to compose.

But it was done now. Her decision had been made.

'And it's the right decision,' Emily muttered to herself as she propped the envelope against her desk calendar. 'The *only* decision.'

For how could she continue as Sebastian's housekeeper, now she realised she'd fallen in love with him?

When he returned home tomorrow morning, she would hand him her resignation, then, first thing next Monday morning, she'd ring the employment agency and tell them she was accepting the job she'd been offered that afternoon.

In truth, Emily had been taken aback at securing such a plum position after just one interview: assistant manager at an exciting new conference centre on Sydney's prestigious Darling Harbour. Which was why, when the agency had rung her just after five today, she'd asked for the weekend to make up her mind.

But she hadn't needed the weekend. Just a couple of hours of soul-searching, plus listening to her head instead of her foolish female heart.

Of course, Sebastian's being away had helped with her decision making. She certainly wasn't looking forward to his return tomorrow, especially after he found out she was leaving.

He was not going to be pleased. Not pleased at all.

Emily knew that Sebastian liked her. Made no

secret of his liking her. That was what made it all so hard, her heart squeezing tight as she recalled the many evenings he'd invited her to sit with him over dinner, or a night-cap, clearly enjoying her company.

But not as much as you enjoyed his, came the timely warning. What Sebastian likes most about you, my girl, is the smoothly efficient way you run his house.

Sebastian liked employees who did what he wanted, when he wanted, the way he wanted. When his much valued PA had tendered her resignation last year, Sebastian had offered her every incentive to make her stay with him. More money. Better working conditions. Even a different title.

Nothing had worked. The woman had left anyway and Sebastian had been in a black mood for days. No, weeks!

Emily quivered inside at the prospect of her boss's reaction to her own resignation.

No doubt he would first offer her more money.

But more money would not persuade her to stay.

Better working conditions would not be possible either, she thought as she glanced around her beautifully furnished bedroom. The desk she was sitting at was made in rosewood, with the most elegantly carved legs. And her four-poster mahogany bed had once been slept in by a European princess. The rest of the one-bedroomed flat which came with her present position was just as exquisite, full of even more antiques, plus many elegant little touches that any female would love. She especially liked the flat's position above the garages, which meant she had total privacy from the main house.

Emily shook her head regretfully. She was really going to miss living here.

But not enough to make her stay.

As for offering her a new title...

There weren't many other ways of describing a housekeeper.

Domestic goddess, perhaps? Emily ventured wryly.

A musical chiming coming from the adjoining living room had Emily glancing at her watch. Eight o'clock. Time to go over to the house and check all the doors and windows, a job she always did every evening around this time when Sebastian was away. She found it impossible to settle down for the night till she felt certain everything was safe and secure.

Picking up her set of keys from where they lay on her desk, Emily headed for the front door of her flat, startled to find, once she stepped outside, that the night air was still very warm. Obviously, the predicted southerly change hadn't arrived yet.

She stood there for a long moment, staring over at Sebastian's house, saddened by the thought that this might be the last time she would do this.

It was such a beautiful house, a Georgian style sandstone mansion sitting on an acre of land on the Hunter's Hill peninsula overlooking the Parramatta River. Originally built in eighteen eighty, the house had been in serious disrepair when Sebastian had bought it several years ago. He'd had it lovingly restored, filling the grand rooms with antiques and adding a conservatory and heated swimming pool.

Upstairs, there were four spacious bedrooms and two bathrooms, one being the private domain of the palatial master bedroom. Downstairs, all the rooms had French windows leading out on to coolly shaded verandas. On the left side of the hallway as you entered, sat a formal reception room which led into an equally formal dining room, which in turn led into the sunny and much more casually furnished conservatory. On the right side of the front hallway, the first door opened into a billiard room. Next along was Sebastian's study-cum-library, followed by the kitchen and utility room.

Out the back was a sunny flagstoned courtyard, a perfect setting for the new swimming pool. On the courtyard's left was a row of golden pines, which gave privacy and acted as a wind-break. On its right, set back a little from the house, were the garages, Emily's flat above reached by way of a flight of steps attached to the side of the stone building, with a small landing at the top on which Emily was currently standing.

Beyond the pool, the beautifully kept lawns fell away in a gentle slope to the river bank, where there was a boathouse and a jetty. Beyond the bank at this point, the river widened into a great expanse of water. In the distance, directly opposite Sebastian's property, the arch of the Gladesville Bridge formed a wonderful backdrop for what was already a mag- nificent view. At this time of night, the lights on the bridge, and the city lights beyond, created a magical and rather romantic atmosphere.

Emily had fallen in love with the place on her very first day.

Falling in love with Sebastian had taken longer, she conceded as she started walking slowly down the steps. In truth, Emily hadn't realised she had till he'd announced one day about a month back that he and his supermodel girlfriend had parted company, with Lana planning to marry an Italian count whom she'd met during a recent fashion week in Milan.

Emily's over-the-top pleasure at this news had been very telling, as had her fierce regret that she'd down-played her looks to secure the job as Sebastian Armstrong's housekeeper. At the time, she'd desperately wanted *any* job and had been advised that Australia's most eligible bachelor was unlikely to hire a thirty-three-year-old blonde with a pretty face and a provocative figure.

Apparently, the mobile phone magnate had been trying to find a suitable housekeeper for some weeks and had expressed his displeasure at the number of applicants so far who'd waltzed into their interviews looking far too glamorous and sexy!

Putting her age up a couple of years, dyeing her hair back to its natural mid-brown, donning glasses and wearing loosely fitting clothes had done the trick: Emily had secured the job.

She'd managed to get rid of the glasses after a few weeks, pretending to take Sebastian's advice to have laser treatment on her eyes. But she'd kept the brown hair, with its plain, pulled-back style, along with the sensible clothes.

Till this last week.

Emily knew better than to go to an interview for a job in the corporate world looking dowdy. So she'd had her shoulder-length hair expertly blow-dried and styled for the occasion. And she'd bought herself a figure-hugging power suit in camel suede, teaming it with a cream cami which showed a hint of cleavage.

Sebastian would hardly have recognised her.

Maybe if she…

'No, no,' Emily muttered to herself as she marched along the covered walkway which skirted the pool and led to the back of the house. 'He'll never look at you in that way no matter what you do, so don't go there.'

Emily valiantly put aside all thought of Sebastian— plus her non-existent chances of attracting him—till she found herself upstairs in his bedroom. Hard not to think of the man when faced with the intimate setting of his love life, not to mention the lingering scent of the woman responsible for her boss's absence.

Ever since Emily had been in Sebastian's employ, there'd only been the one woman in his life: Lana Campbell. In her late twenties, Lana was currently at the height of her modelling career, in great demand for catwalk work, especially in Italy. A natural redhead, she was statuesque and curvy. The Italians did not like skinny models. Although not traditionally beautiful, Lana was exotic-looking, with startling green eyes and a sultry mouth. She was also extremely intelligent, with a sharp wit which could tip over into sarcasm if she didn't like you.

She didn't like Emily, for some reason. Though she'd been clever enough to hide that dislike from Sebastian.

She also had a temper. In the weeks leading up to their break-up, Emily had often overheard Lana being very vocal in her complaints about their relationship.

Sebastian didn't love her, she'd screamed at him on one occasion. If he did, he would marry her. Or at least let her move in with him.

He wouldn't do either, for whatever reason. Neither would he be provoked.

Sebastian was not a man to ever raise his voice. He had other ways of showing his displeasure. Whenever Lana made a scene, he would look at her coldly and then walk away, after which she would inevitably storm off.

But Emily felt certain that Sebastian did love Lana, a fact confirmed when he'd flown to Italy five days ago, clearly in an attempt to get her back. Not successfully, as it had turned out.

Lana's wedding to the Italian count had gone ahead a couple of days ago, and had been extensively covered by the media.

Sebastian had emailed Emily the following day, his message curt and brief.

Landing Mascot Saturday morning at seven. Home by eight.

Usually his emails to Emily were a bit more friendly. Clearly, he was going to be in a difficult frame of mind when he returned. Not a pleasant prospect.

Still, losing the woman he loved to another man was never going to sit well with him. Although heaven only knew what Lana saw in that Italian count. Compared to Sebastian, he was downright ugly: very short and decidedly overweight, with a weak fleshy face and beady black eyes.

Of course, he had a title. And he *had* presented Lana with a wedding ring.

Sebastian couldn't really expect a girl like that to settle for less. Lana probably wanted children as well as marriage. Clearly, Sebastian didn't.

It was obvious to Emily that her forty-year-old single employer liked his life the way it was. Liked his space. Liked being alone sometimes. Australian men could be like that.

Italians, however, were a very gregarious race, renowned for their sense of family and love of children.

Thinking about family and children reaffirmed Emily's decision.

Yes, it was definitely time to leave. Time to actively pursue the future Emily also wanted for herself. Which was a husband and at least one child before she was too old.

Eighteen months ago, Emily hadn't given a damn about marriage and babies. Or about men. She'd still been grief-stricken over her mother's death from cancer. And devastated by the discovery of her father's betrayal.

But time had a way of changing your mind about things; wounds could heal and priorities change. Emily could understand why Lana had left Sebastian to marry her Italian count. Passion and sex were not the be-all and end-all to a woman, although Emily would have found it extremely hard to leave Sebastian's bed.

'Just as well you've never been in it, then,' she snapped irritably to herself when her eyes kept being drawn to that very bed. 'You're having enough trouble leaving the man as it is!'

But leave him I will, Emily vowed, as she hurried from the room.

No more being a martyr for you, my girl!

Okay, so she was in love with the man. Big deal. She'd been in love before. With that rat, Mark, who'd jumped ship when she'd gone home to nurse her mother.

Surely she could fall in love again, she reassured herself as she headed down the stairs.

First, however, she had to get herself out of here and out there, into a different world than the cloistered environment she was currently living in. A conference centre would bring her into contact with oodles of eligible executive types every day. If she had her hair dyed an eye-catching blonde again and invested in a new figure-hugging wardrobe, she was sure to attract plenty of male attention. It would just be a matter of weeding out the creeps and finding a quality man with a good job who was capable of true caring and a solid commitment.

And if he wasn't quite as impressive as Sebastian, then that was too bad. Not too many men were.

Sebastian was a man amongst men. Strikingly handsome, with a brilliant mind, a great body, and more passions than any man Emily had ever met. Aside from his various business achievements, he was an accomplished sportsman, as well as an expert in antiques, and wine, and whatever subject currently took his fancy. His library was extensive, with books on a wide variety of topics, along with a huge array of biographies. He'd told her once that he found inspiration from reading about the lives of successful people: people who'd forged their own paths and made their own luck in life.

'And that's just what *I'm* going to do, Sebastian,' Emily announced as she locked the back door. 'Forge my own path and make my own luck!'

Despite all her common sense lecturings and brave resolves, by the time Emily reached her flat, her insides were totally twisted up into knots. Going to bed was not an option. Too early. Neither was watching TV. She'd grown bored with the television lately, becoming sick and tired of reality shows.

Reading didn't appeal, either.

Perhaps a swim…

She'd already had a swim earlier in the afternoon, Sydney having experienced the longest, hottest summer on record. Today it had been thirty-one degrees, despite summer having given way to autumn three weeks back. The water in the solar-heated pool would still be warm, and very inviting.

Emily made her way straight to the bathroom, where she stripped off all her sensible housekeeping clothes and reached for her black one-piece swimming costume, which was draped over the claw-footed bath. It was still wet and Emily grimaced at the thought of dragging the wet Lycra over her warm body.

The temptation to go skinny-dipping popped into her head.

Strangely enough, Emily had never been skinny-dipping. Yet she'd been a bit of a wild child in her teens, and a real party animal in her twenties.

What had happened to that girl? she wondered as she pushed the temptation aside, then started to step into the wet swimming costume.

'She's in danger of turning into an old maid, that's what,' Emily muttered. 'And an old fuddy-duddy to boot!'

That did it!

Throwing the damp costume back across the bath, Emily snatched down the white towelling robe which she kept on a hook high on the bathroom door. Rebellion fuelled her actions as she shoved her arms into the roomy sleeves and sashed the robe around her naked body.

But her courage faded once she was out by the pool and faced with the prospect of actually taking that robe off. She stood there for ages, reassuring herself that the pool had total privacy from prying neighbours and there was no one else in the house to see her.

Sebastian didn't like his household staff to live in. Only Emily. A cleaner came in on Mondays and Fridays to do the heavy cleaning. And Emily hired casual staff to help her whenever Sebastian entertained. A local garden and landscaping service looked after the grounds and a pool man came in once a week to keep the water sparkling clean.

Emily had no reason to feel nervous about having a dip without any clothes on. No one was going to pop up unexpectedly, especially her employer.

In Emily's experience, Sebastian was a very predictable man, addicted to routine and punctuality. If he said he would arrive in the morning, then that was when he would arrive.

Yet when Emily finally took off the towelling robe, her eyes kept darting up to the blackened windows of the house, worried that a light would suddenly snap on upstairs and Sebastian would be standing there at his bedroom window looking down at her.

Agitated by this thought, Emily swiftly stepped up to the side of the pool, stretched out her hands and dived into the water, not surfacing till she was halfway up the thirty-metre pool. As she slicked back her hair with her hands, she once again glanced nervously up at Sebastian's bedroom window, relieved to find it still in darkness.

The pool was not in darkness, however; some subtle underwater lighting shone through the crystal clear water. Emily felt both vulnerable and exposed as she began the rather amazing experience of swimming in the nude. The water was like warm silk caressing her unclothed flesh, bringing an acute awareness of her female body.

Swimming breast-stroke was a definite turn-on, something Emily didn't need at that precise moment. Because being turned on made her think of Sebastian and the sexual longings he'd begun to inspire in her.

Lately, she'd found herself day-dreaming about him all the time, wondering what it would be like to be his girlfriend, to have him look at her the way she'd seen him look at Lana—with white-hot desire blazing bright in his brilliantly blue eyes.

Emily abruptly changed to the more vigorous overarm, swimming with rapid strokes and her head down till she reached the far end of the pool. Gripping the curved terracotta tiles at the edge, she sucked in some much-needed air, once again lecturing herself on the futility of her love for her boss.

The sooner she was away from that man, the better!

Emily pushed herself back from the side of the pool, staying on her back, gently moving her arms to stop herself from sinking. Floating that way was not quite so erotic, providing she didn't look down at her generous breasts and their disturbingly erect peaks. Impossible to blame their state on being cold. More likely she was too hot from thinking about Sebastian.

Emily directed her gaze steadfastly upwards, at the night sky above. It was inky black and star-studded. The moon was only a quarter, but how brightly it shone. A night for lovers, or for witches.

The security lights near the house suddenly snapping on had Emily jerking upright with a gasp. Spinning round in the water sent a great mass of wet hair across her face, so she couldn't make out who it was standing at the edge of the pool. But she recognised his voice from the very first word.

'What in the hell do you think you're doing, Missie, swimming in my pool without any clothes on?'

CHAPTER TWO

SEBASTIAN. Oh, my God, it was Sebastian!

What cruel twist of fate would bring him home early on the one night she'd decided to go skinny-dipping?

Emily didn't know what to do. Whether to use her hands to cover her breasts, or push the hair off her face, so that he could recognise who it was swimming in his pool.

'I'm waiting for an answer, Missie,' Sebastian snapped.

His calling her Missie like that evoked some much-needed resentment that she'd been put in this humiliating situation. Was it her fault that he'd come home early?

Absolutely not!

Piqued, Emily dipped her head forward in the water, then threw it backwards, the action sending her hair flying back off her face and plastering it to her bare back.

Fortunately, she was far enough away for the spray of water created not to hit Sebastian, who was standing at the edge of the pool, his trousered legs wide apart, his dark suit jacket pushed back, his hands on his hips.

He still didn't seem to recognise her, despite her whole face now being exposed.

Understandable, Emily conceded ruefully, considering he was glaring down at what else was exposed.

'It's only me, Sebastian,' she said, sounding much cooler than she felt.

Sebastian's eyes jerked up to hers, his darkly frowning expression immediately changing to bewilderment, before settling on shock.

'Emily? My God, it *is* you!'

Emily's face flamed when his eyes dropped back down to her naked breasts. She valiantly resisted the urge to cover them, pride demanding that she brazen things out rather than start acting like a shy, simpering virgin.

Besides, there was something satisfying in seeing Sebastian stare at her like that. Emily knew she had a good body. Now Sebastian knew it too.

But it was a perverse satisfaction. Because it inevitably turned to distress.

'I didn't expect you home,' she said somewhat stiffly, pained at the way he couldn't seem to take his eyes off her breasts.

Men could be so shallow when it came to sex, she thought bitterly. Even Sebastian.

'Obviously not,' he said, his gaze drifting even lower in the water.

Her chin tilted upwards as defiance kicked in. 'I'd like to get out now,' she threw at him.

'Pity. I was just thinking of joining you.'

'*What?*'

'Nothing like a relaxing swim after a long flight.'

His sudden shrugging off of his jacket and tossing it carelessly aside brought Emily close to panic. Surely he couldn't mean to strip off and go skinny-dipping with her. Surely not!

'Have…have you been drinking?' she blurted out shakily.

He smiled a slightly crooked smile as he dispensed with his tie, then attacked the buttons on his blue business shirt. 'First class flying does come with the very best of wine.'

So he *had* been drinking. Which accounted for this most uncharacteristic behaviour. In all the months she'd worked for Sebastian, he'd never crossed that invisible line between employer and employee. Even when she'd sat with him at dinner time, they hadn't talked of personal or private things, their conversation restricted to more general topics. He'd never said or done anything which could have been misconstrued or would give offence.

Clearly, he wasn't himself tonight. Losing Lana must have unhinged him.

'It's never a good idea to drink and swim, Sebastian,' she pointed out, not unkindly.

'You'll be here to save me.'

'No, I won't. I just told you. I'm getting out now.'

'What if I ask you to stay?'

Emily groaned. If only he knew how much she'd like to stay.

But she wasn't about to be used, not even by him.

'I'm not comfortable with this, Sebastian,' she said quite sharply.

He stopped undressing, his eyes narrowing on her. His sigh, when it came, sounded weary.

'You're right,' he said. 'I'm behaving badly. Please forgive me.'

Before she could utter a single word of forgiveness, or anything else, he snatched up his jacket from the ground, whirled on his heel and was gone, disappearing through the back door.

Emily wasted no time, swimming over to the side of the pool, scrambling out and dragging her robe on over her dripping body. She flew across the pool surrounds and along the flagstone walkway, running up the steps and inside her flat, slamming the door behind her.

Only then did she realise she was shaking. Not from fear. From how incredibly stupid she'd just been!

She clasped her hands to her head as she realised how close she'd just come to having her wildest fantasy come true—that of having Sebastian make love to her.

If and when a male and female went skinny-dipping together, it was never a platonic activity. Sebastian might not have looked at her with quite the same passion as he'd once looked at Lana, but there had definitely been desire in his eyes as they'd raked over her naked body. No doubt about that!

Okay, so it would have been nothing but sex on his part, Emily conceded. She would have just been a substitute for Lana, a salve for his male ego.

But so what? her love-sick soul protested. She would have known what it was like to be in his arms, to have him kiss her and touch her. She could have *pretended*, at least for a little while.

And now?

Now, all she had was frustration and regret. And her stupid bloody pride!

Tears rushed into her eyes. Why, oh, why couldn't she have thrown caution to the wind? Why did she have to be so damned self-righteous?

Any other female would have taken what was on offer. And who knew? Something might have come of it, something special. She had a lot to offer Sebastian.

But he has nothing special to offer you in return, the voice of reason intervened. Not love…Or marriage…Or children.

Only sex.

You had a lucky escape tonight, my girl. Now hand in your resignation in the morning, then get the hell out of here!

CHAPTER THREE

THE pre-set alarm on Sebastian's bedside clock went off at ten to six. He woke with a start, followed by a groan.

Despite having found oblivion the moment his head had hit the pillow last night, and sleeping a good nine hours, he'd resurfaced this morning with a slight hangover, his first in years.

Still, he only had himself to blame. He'd drunk far too much during the flight home, though goodness knew he'd had to do something to block out the memory of what had happened in Milan.

It had worked too.

By the time the plane had landed at Mascot, Lana had been consigned to history and all he'd wanted was to get himself home.

And what had happened?

He'd arrived to find his ladylike housekeeper skinny-dipping in his pool, showing off the sort of body which he'd always found a serious turn-on.

Not that he'd recognised her at first. He'd thought

she was some wild young chicky-babe from the neighbourhood.

The moment he'd realised it was Emily, however, he should have reined in his galloping hormones. Instead, his behaviour had bordered on sexual harassment.

Fortunately, his very sensible housekeeper had put him right back in his place, saving him from the embarrassment of doing something he would very definitely have regretted this morning. As much as he had been momentarily struck by desire for Emily, he valued her far too much to risk losing her.

Thankfully, she'd noted that he'd been drinking and hadn't seemed too offended. Though she'd made him feel like a naughty schoolboy with her rather pointed remarks.

He still felt chastened this morning. And somewhat perplexed. How could he not have noticed those incredible breasts before?

As Sebastian threw back the bed-clothes and struggled out of bed, he wondered if she did that kind of thing often. Went skinny-dipping, that was. It seemed extremely out of character.

Still, she had every right to do as she pleased when he was away. And every right to expect her employer to always act like a gentleman around her, no matter what the circumstances. Or the provocations.

Although apologies did not come easily to Sebastian's lips, he decided to say sorry again over breakfast this morning.

In the meantime, he had to get himself dressed and down to the river. It was time for his morning exercise.

Exercise always cleared his head. That, and the two painkillers he intended to take right now.

Emily stood at her bedroom window, watching Sebastian as he strode down the path which led to the boathouse, his black wetsuit protecting him from the cooler air which had swept into Sydney shortly after midnight. Dawn was just breaking, the sky turning from purple to that soft blue-grey which often preceded the sun bursting over the horizon.

Emily admired Sebastian's dedication to his morning fitness regime, but she sometimes wondered if he bordered on being a bit obsessive. One would think that after yesterday's long flight home—plus a possible hangover—he might have given it a miss this morning.

But no! There he was, striding forth down to the water's edge, as he did every morning right on six.

Clearly, he'd slept well last night and wasn't suffering any jet-lag, or other after-effects. His broad shoulders were back, his handsome head held high. He looked simply superb.

'Oh, Sebastian,' she murmured, before turning abruptly away from the window.

How could just *looking* at the man give her pleasure? It was perverse in the extreme, as perverse as the pleasure she'd felt when he'd looked at her last night.

Love did make fools of people—women, especially.

Thinking such thoughts gave Emily the courage to go through with what she'd decided to do last night.

And to face the inevitably unpleasant confrontation with Sebastian after she'd tendered her resignation.

An hour later she was in the process of setting the breakfast table in the conservatory when she heard the back door open and close. The master of the house had returned as he always did right on seven. Fortunately, he always went straight back upstairs to shower and shave. In thirty minutes, however, he'd be back downstairs and she'd be facing the music.

Her stomach tightened as she anticipated Sebastian's reaction to her resignation letter. She'd weakly decided to put it on the breakfast table, rather than hand it to him personally.

At seven-thirty Emily was standing next to the coffee percolator, rehearsing her speech over why she was leaving when the hairs on the back of her neck suddenly stood up. She knew, before she spun around on her sensible trainers, that Sebastian would be standing in the doorway.

He was, looking his usual sophisticated self, in smart fawn trousers and a long-sleeved black and cream striped shirt.

Emily tried to stop her stupid heart from pounding at the sight of him. But without much success.

'Yes?' she said a bit sharply, thinking irritably that no man had a right to have so many attractions.

'I wanted to apologise again about last night,' he said in his richly masculine voice. 'I was way out of line.'

'It's okay, Sebastian,' she returned somewhat stiffly. 'No harm done.'

His dark brows drew together into a frown. 'Are you sure? You seem a bit...out of sorts...this morning.'

'I'm just embarrassed.'

'You have nothing to be embarrassed over.'

'You weren't supposed to come home till this morning,' she said, half accusingly.

'I caught an earlier flight than I intended.'

'You shocked the life out of me.'

'I was pretty shocked myself, to find a naked nymph in my pool. I didn't recognise you without your clothes on.'

Emily winced. 'Please, Sebastian, couldn't we just forget about last night?'

'If that's what you want...'

'It is.'

'Fine,' he said matter-of-factly. 'I won't be having a cooked breakfast this morning. Just toast. Bring the coffee in as soon as it's ready, will you?' he added. And was gone.

Emily closed her eyes and waited for the summons which she knew would come very very shortly.

'Emily, would you come in here, please?' came the gruff call from the conservatory less than thirty seconds later.

Leaving the coffee to perc by itself, Emily straightened her shoulders and headed in the direction of the conservatory, her hands curling into fists by her sides.

Don't let him talk you out of leaving, she lectured herself as she made her way through the dining room. *Keep focused. And strong.*

The double doors which separated the dining room from the conservatory were wide open, as they always were every morning. Sebastian's back was to her as she walked through, but the set of his head and shoulders were intimidating, to say the least. Emily knew, before she saw the formidable expression on his face, that he was not happy.

But that was no surprise.

'What's the meaning of this?' he snapped as soon as she moved into sight. Her resignation letter was in his right hand, opened and obviously read. 'I thought you said you were okay with last night.'

Emily scooped in a deeply gathering breath, exhaling slowly as she uncurled her fists and looped her hands together in front of her in an attitude of superbly feigned composure.

'My resigning had nothing to do with last night, Sebastian,' she told him calmly. 'I had already typed out that letter *before* you came home. I've been offered another job and I've decided to take it.'

'Another job?' he repeated, managing to sound both startled and affronted. 'What other job? I sincerely hope none of my so-called friends have poached you from me,' he added, his eyes the colour of a stormy sky.

'I have not taken another housekeeping position,' Emily was relieved to inform him. 'I'm to be the assistant manager at a new conference centre at Darling Harbour. If you recall from my résumé, I have a degree in Hospitality Management. I also worked for several years at the Regency Hotel on their front desk, and in their PR department, so I am well qualified for such a position.'

He looked at her hard for several seconds whilst he slowly slapped her letter against the palm of his left hand. Finally, he stopped the irritating action and placed her letter down on the table whilst his lips made tight little movements back and forth, outer evidence of an inner anger which he was battling to contain.

'And how did this offer come about?' he asked in clipped tones.

'I put my name down at an employment agency. They sent me for an interview on Thursday, then rang me yesterday afternoon to offer me the job.'

'On just the one interview? You must have impressed them.'

'Apparently so.'

'You've been planning to leave for a while, I take it? From what I know of the corporate world, you don't even get an interview like that overnight.'

'I've been looking for another position for a few weeks.'

'Why, Emily? I thought you were happy here.'

'I have been happy here.'

His expression showed confusion. 'Is it the money, then? You want more money?'

'No. I don't want more money.'

'You want more time off?'

'No. I have plenty of time off, Sebastian, with you being away on business every second week or so.'

'Then what is it that you want, Emily? You must know I'll do anything in my power to keep you.'

Emily had known he'd take this tack. But she was ready for him.

'You can't give me what I want, Sebastian.'

'Try me.'

'I want to marry and have a family before I'm too old. I'll be thirty-five next birthday, and…'

'Wait a minute there,' he interjected brusquely. 'If I recall rightly, you were already thirty-six when you applied for *this* job. That makes you going on thirty-eight, not thirty-five.'

Emily sighed. Trust her to make that mistake. But the cat was out of the bag. No point in trying any further cover-ups.

'I didn't think you'd hire me if you knew I was only thirty-three. So I increased my age by three years.'

'I see. And what other subterfuges did you do to get me to hire you?'

Emily pulled a face. What did it matter if she told him the total truth now?

'I was advised by the agency not to look too glamorous, so I dyed my hair a mousy brown and wore glasses. And yes, I lied to you about having laser treatment later. I found I simply couldn't stand wearing glasses.'

'Understandable. That's why I had laser treatment on my own eyes.'

When he leant back in the chair and began studying her rather closely, Emily had to use her well practised—and often pretend—composure to stay calm and still. But inside she wanted to run from the way his eyes travelled over her. Because they were undressing her, stripping her of her loosely fitted navy tracksuit and seeing her as they'd seen her last night. Without a stitch of clothes on.

It took all of Emily's will power not to blush.

'So what *is* your natural hair colour?' he asked at last.

'Actually, mousy brown *is* my natural hair colour,' she said, proud of her steady voice and direct gaze. 'But I've been dyeing it blonde ever since I was sixteen.'

'I see. Presumably, before you came to work for me, your wardrobe was somewhat more flattering as well. As much as you might want me to forget last night, it was impossible not to notice that you do have a very...delectable...shape.'

Heat zoomed into her cheeks. She couldn't help it.

'I didn't care what I looked like at the time.'

'But you do now...'

'Yes. Yes, I do now.'

'Because you want to find yourself a husband.'

'Yes.'

'You feel you can't do that while you work for me?'

'Come now, Sebastian, I'll *never* meet a potential husband if I stay here, in this job. Maybe you haven't noticed, but I don't have a social life. I don't have any friends. That's been my choice up till now, I admit. When I took this job, I needed to retreat from the outside world. I needed time to heal.'

'I presume you're talking about your mother's death.'

Emily frowned before recalling she'd mentioned her mother's death at her initial job interview. She'd had to explain what she'd been doing during the years leading up to her applying for the housekeeping job.

'That,' she said, 'and other things.'

'What other things?'

Emily was beginning to find his persistence very annoying. 'That's my private and personal business.'

His face reflected some hurt at her curtly delivered rebuke. 'I thought we'd become friends during your time here, Emily,' he said with disarming softness.

Emily squirmed a little. 'Please, Sebastian, don't make this harder for me than it already is.'

'You don't really want to leave, do you?'

Emily tried not to let him see the truth in her eyes. But she suspected she failed.

'I don't want you to leave either,' he said. 'You are the best housekeeper I've ever had. You make it a pleasure for me to come home.'

Oh, God…

'I *have* to move on, Sebastian.'

'Rubbish!' he said, snapping forward on his chair. 'You don't have to do any such thing. There must be a way around this problem where we can both have what we want.'

'I don't see how.'

He stared at her for a long moment before a light suddenly switched on in his blue eyes. The sort of light which came with an idea.

'We'll talk about it over lunch,' he announced.

Emily sighed an exasperated sigh. 'Sebastian, you are not going to get me to change my mind.'

'Give me the opportunity to try.'

'If you insist.'

'I insist.'

Emily's teeth clenched hard in her jaw. He really was an impossible man!

'What would you like for lunch?' she asked coolly, determined not to let him rattle her.

'I'll be taking you out to lunch, Emily.'

She blinked, then just stared at him whilst her heart flipped over inside her chest. So much for her resolve not to be rattled.

'And I want you to dress the way you dressed when you got that fancy new job,' he added, his eyes taking on a knowing gleam.

'*What?*'

'I'm sure you didn't snare such a position looking the way you look this morning. Now, I have some business to attend to in the city after breakfast, but I'll be back by noon. We'll leave at twelve-thirty.'

'You're wasting your time, Sebastian,' she said, desperate now to hold on to what little of her composure was left.

'I never waste my time, Emily,' he returned in a voice which sent an odd chill running down her spine.

Suddenly, she was afraid. Afraid that by the end of lunch she would forget her own sensible plans and do exactly whatever Sebastian suggested.

'That coffee smells good,' he went on abruptly and picked up the morning paper. 'You'd better bring it in before the percolator boils dry.'

CHAPTER FOUR

By NINE o'clock Sebastian had left for wherever he was going in the city. Probably his office, Emily reasoned, since he drove off in his car, a silver Maserati Spyder which matched its owner for style and power, but required careful parking, especially in the city.

The office of Armstrong Industries was situated in a high rise building in the middle of Sydney's CBD, which had its own underground car park and which supplied a number of parking spaces to the lessees of its office space.

The executives at Armstrong Industries didn't have to catch trains and buses to work. Nor did they have to pay the exorbitant fees charged by public car parks in the city. Their jobs came with their own personal car spot as a highly prized perk.

As CEO and owner of the company, Sebastian had two private parking spaces.

Emily knew this because Sebastian had offered her the use of one of them last year, not long before

Christmas, after she'd complained about the horren-
dous parking situation in the city. When she'd thanked
him for his kind offer, Lana—who'd been staying
over at the time—had caustically remarked that
Sebastian's occasional bursts of generosity always
had an ulterior motive and she'd better watch herself.

Whilst Emily could not possibly see what ulterior
motive Sebastian could have had on that occasion,
she had to privately agree that her boss was basically
self-absorbed, as a lot of successful men were.

So she knew Sebastian's reasons for taking her to
lunch today would be entirely selfish ones. He didn't
really care about what she wanted. Only about what *he*
wanted. Which was her, staying on as his housekeeper.

His asking her to doll herself up for their lunch
date was a puzzle, however. Unless he didn't want to
be embarrassed by being seen in public with a
woman who looked downright dowdy. Which she
did this morning, in her less than flattering tracksuit
and with her hair pulled back into a knot.

What would Sebastian think, Emily wondered as
she completed her household chores, when he saw
her wearing her smart new suede suit and with her
hair done properly and full make-up on?

Would he be shocked?

She hoped so. She hoped he'd be stopped in his
tracks.

Emily craved the opportunity to show him that she
was an attractive woman. Maybe not as glamorous
or as sexy as Lana, but still capable of attracting male
attention.

As nervous as she was about this lunch, she now had her chance. And she aimed to make the most of it!

Noon saw Emily looking the best she could without going blonde, but with more butterflies in her stomach than when she'd gone for her job interview the other day. She kept worrying over what arguments Sebastian was going to employ to persuade her to stay, her improved appearance no longer the main focus of her thoughts.

The sudden sound of the garage door opening underneath her flat sent her running towards the window which overlooked the driveway. She reached it just in time to see the top of Sebastian's sports car disappearing into the garages below, the heavy door automatically coming down behind it.

His putting his car away brought confusion and dismay. Did that mean he'd changed his mind about taking her to lunch? Had he decided she wasn't worth the effort of trying to change her mind?

Emily was still standing at the window, feeling totally crestfallen, when there was a knock at her door. It would be Sebastian, of course, she thought unhappily, come to tell her lunch was off.

Steeling herself not to act like some disappointed fool, she went to answer it. But inside, Emily fiercely regretted the time she'd taken to painstakingly blow-dry her hair the way the hairdresser had the other day, practically strand by strand. It had taken ages. So had her make-up. What a waste of time!

After scooping in one last calming breath, she swept open the door, her face an impassive mask.

Sebastian wasn't exactly stopped in his tracks by the sight of her.

But he did take a long look.

'Just as I thought,' he said, his eyes showing satisfaction as they raked over her from top to toe. 'You're no plain Jane, are you, Emily? Not that I ever thought you were. Impossible to hide your lovely skin and eyes. As for your stunning figure...I confess you have hidden that extremely well these past eighteen months. But last night rather put paid to that little subterfuge.'

Emily struggled to prevent an embarrassing blush from spoiling her resolve to remain cool and calm, no matter what.

'It's nice to finally see your curves shown to advantage,' he added, his gaze dropping to the hint of cleavage displayed by the lowishly-cut camisole.

Emily froze when her nipples tightened alarmingly within the silk confines of her strapless bra. No, she thought angrily. No, no, no!

Time to stop this little scenario before it became seriously humiliating.

'Thank you,' she replied frostily. 'I take it you've changed your mind about lunch?'

Her assumption surprised him more than her appearance had, his head jerking back as his brows drew together in a startled frown. 'Why would you say that?'

'You put your car away.'

'Aah. I see. No, I've ordered us a taxi. Easier than trying to park at the Quay. It'll be here at twelve-thirty, so I'd better away and change into something more suitable for lunching with such a beautiful lady.'

It was no use. This time she did blush. And it irritated the life out of her. As did the degree of her relief—and delight—that their lunch together was still on.

'Flattery won't change my mind, Sebastian,' she said sharply.

'Thank you for warning me. But I would never rely on flattery for something so important as keeping you, Emily.'

Emily squared her shoulders in defiance of the supreme confidence she saw in his eyes. 'There's no point in offering me more money, either. Or better working conditions.'

'Look, let's leave this discussion till later. The taxi is due in twenty minutes. What say we meet on the front veranda just before twelve-thirty?'

Emily sighed. 'Very well.'

'There's no need to sound so put out. At worst, you will have a free lunch. At best...' He shrugged, obviously not willing as yet to reveal his battle plans. 'Must go. See you shortly.'

Emily shook her head as she closed the door behind his departing back. Sebastian meant to persuade her to stay. How he aimed to achieve that goal was the unsettling question.

As the minutes ticked down to their arranged meeting on the front veranda, the thought haunted Emily that there was no such thing as a free lunch.

At twelve twenty-five, she picked up the camel-coloured handbag which matched her suit, locked her apartment door, then made her way downstairs, each step reminding her of the tightness of her skirt and the height of her heels.

Whilst more than happy with her smart city-girl look, Emily was relieved that her suit jacket covered most of her breasts, and her still erect nipples. Thankfully, the morning had not warmed up too much, despite the sky being clear and sunny, so she could keep the covering jacket on without feeling too hot.

Locking the back door of the main house on her way through didn't take long, Emily telling herself all the time to keep calm and not let Sebastian change her mind about leaving, no matter what he said.

But it wasn't what he would *say*, came the unsettling realisation when she walked out on to the front veranda to find him already waiting for her. It was the way he could make her *feel*.

Emily already knew that just looking at him gave her pleasure.

Being taken to lunch by him, however, was a whole different ball game. She would have to keep her wits about her.

He looked superb, of course, dressed in an elegant grey business suit, his shirt blue, his tie a silvery grey. His slicked-back dark brown hair looked faintly damp, suggesting he'd had a quick shower. He might have run a razor over his chin as well, as the skin on his face looked very smooth and sleek.

'I love a lady who knows how to be on time,' he said with a quick smile. 'Did you lock the back door?'

'Of course,' came her cool reply.

'Of course,' he repeated. Not nastily. Or sarcastically.

But it annoyed her just the same.

'The taxi's here,' she pointed out, nodding towards the front gates, which were shut. Sebastian often caught taxis but never let them come inside. He valued his privacy, and his security.

Understandable, considering the extent of his wealth.

'I'll just lock the front door,' he said.

Emily practised some deep breathing while he did so.

When he turned and took her arm, she flinched before she could stop herself.

'Come now, Emily,' came his smooth rebuke. 'I'm not going to bite.'

The penny dropped. So this was how he was going to persuade her to stay. By using his not inconsiderable charm. His demanding that she get dressed up was an underhand but clever way of making her more aware of her femininity, thereby lowering her sexual defences.

And it was working, of course.

'I still can't get over how amazing you look,' he continued as he steered her down the front steps and along the front path. 'But you're right, I think you'd look even better with blonde hair. One of those short sexy styles which would show off your swan-like neck.'

The deviousness of his tactics inspired rebellion, as did the traitorous heat which his touch was sending through her entire body.

'I'll keep that in mind before I start my new job,' she told him in a brilliantly blithe tone.

Not with much effect, however, because he laughed. 'You know, I realised when you were talking this morning that you were just like me.'

'Like *you*?' she threw up at him, stunned by such an unlikely observation.

'Absolutely. You do what has to be done. You don't fantasise or romanticise. You're a realist.'

Their arriving at the front gates stopped Emily from blurting out that he knew nothing about her at all. She'd been fantasising about him for weeks!

Getting through the gates and into the taxi gave her a few moments to become what Sebastian thought she was. A cool-headed realist.

Till they were under way.

Finding herself sitting so close to the man she loved in the confined space of the taxi was not conducive to sensible thinking. The lack of conversation didn't help, either. Suddenly, there was nothing to distract her heated imagination, or to stop it from running amok.

Could he possibly be planning to seduce her? came the horribly exciting thought. Would he go that far to keep her? And if he did proposition her, how would she react?

Last night, she'd regretted not going skinny-dipping with him.

Today, she suspected she might be putty in his hands.

In all seriousness, however, Emily could not

believe Sebastian would go that far. He was not a callous womaniser. Or a cold-blooded seducer. He was a gentleman through and through. That was why she'd been so shocked last night when he'd suggested joining her in the pool.

'Have you officially accepted that new job offer?'

Sebastian's unexpected question whipped her head around, her rapidly blinking eyes taking a moment to focus on his face.

Something in her own face must have betrayed her.

'You haven't, have you?' he said, sounding pleased.

Emily adopted what she hoped was a totally un-ruffled expression. 'I intend ringing the agency first thing Monday morning to accept.'

'Why didn't you accept the offer straight away?'

'I don't like to rush any decision,' she told him coolly and he nodded.

'Sensible girl.'

'That doesn't mean I didn't decide later, Sebastian,' she went on, hammering home her stance. 'That's why I resigned as your housekeeper this morning. In three weeks' time I will no longer be working for you. Trust me on that.'

'I believe you.'

'Then what is the point of this lunch?'

'I intend to make you a counter-offer.'

'What kind of counter-offer?'

He placed his index finger against his lips. 'When we're alone,' he murmured.

She stared at his finger, then at his lips.

Sebastian had a very sensual mouth, in contrast to

the rest of his more harshly sculptured features. His lips were soft and full, whilst his cheekbones were sharply prominent, his nose long and strong, his chin squared and stubborn.

But it was his eyes which dominated his face and inevitably drew one's own eyes. Deeply set and a bright blue, with a darker blue rim, they were piercing and quite magnetic.

Emily found herself looking up and into them; found herself thinking she would do anything he asked, if only he would keep looking at her like this. As if she were an attractive woman. No, a *desirable* woman.

She could not tear her eyes away from his, no longer caring about anything but this moment, this precious, private, impossibly romantic moment.

'Whereabouts around here do you want me to drop you off, mate?' the taxi driver asked.

Sebastian looked away and the moment was gone, torn from Emily with the wrenching pain of a suddenly amputated limb. Reality returned with a rush, making her face the fancifulness of her interpretation of what had just happened, plus what she was secretly hoping might happen later on.

Sebastian was not going to seduce her. He was going to offer her more money.

Her boss was a man who found practical solutions to problems he encountered, not ones which could cause him even more problems. Seducing his housekeeper would be an extremely hazardous solution, especially for a wealthy man. Sebastian would not risk his reputation—or a sexual harassment lawsuit—to keep her in his house. She wasn't *that* valuable to him.

'Just here will do,' Sebastian told the driver, and the taxi slid over to the kerb just outside the ferry terminals.

From there, it was only a short walk down to the restaurants and alfresco cafés which lined the quayside and which all provided their patrons with splendid views of the harbour, the bridge and the Opera House.

Emily had no idea where Sebastian was taking her but she couldn't imagine it being anything less than the best.

Having lunch with him, however, had now totally lost its lustre. She'd be relieved when it was over. *Very* relieved when he graciously accepted her decision to leave.

Emily opened the door and climbed out of the taxi, not waiting for Sebastian to do it for her.

No more mooning over him, she lectured herself as she stood on the pavement and waited for him to finish paying the driver. No more foolish fantasies. No more saying she was going to do one thing whilst dreaming about another.

Be the realist he thinks you are.

'Emily?'

A startled Emily turned at the sound of her name being called out from behind her.

'So it *is* you,' the owner of the male voice said as he strode over to her, his good-looking face breaking into a warm smile. 'I didn't recognise you at first with brown hair.'

CHAPTER FIVE

EMILY could not believe it! Fancy running into Mark, of all people.

Still, he did live at Manly and had always caught the ferry to and from work. And he often worked on a Saturday, being one of the partners in a high-powered stockbroking firm.

She supposed it wasn't all that much of a coincidence.

But still…

'You're looking very well,' Mark went on, his eyes fairly gobbling her up.

'You too,' she replied, privately wishing that he might have grown fat or bald in the four years since he'd dumped her. But no, he looked even better than ever.

Not as tall or as impressive as Sebastian, but extremely attractive. And very well dressed—Mark had always had style. And an eye for the ladies. He was eyeing her up and down right now, his dark eyes glittering in that way she'd once loved, because she'd thought his desire had been just for her.

In hindsight, Emily suspected that he probably looked at every fanciable female with I'd-love-to-take-you-to-bed eyes.

'I've often thought of you, Emily,' he said, lowering his voice in the way she now realised was a ploy he used to sound sincere.

'And I you, Mark.'

He didn't seem to notice the chilly note in her reply.

'Good heavens!' he suddenly exclaimed, his eyes having abruptly moved from her face to a spot over her shoulder. 'That's Sebastian Armstrong over there.'

Emily spun round to see that Sebastian was finally getting out of the taxi.

'Yes, it is,' she agreed coolly. 'He's taking me to lunch.'

Emily enjoyed Mark's shocked expression. 'You're moving in pretty rarefied circles these days.'

'Sebastian's my boss.'

'No kidding. The great man himself. Look, can I give you a call? It'd be great to catch up.'

Emily found it difficult to hide her fury at Mark imagining for one moment that she'd want him calling her. Or catching up with her.

'I don't think so, Mark,' she said frostily.

'No? Oh, well, I suppose you've got better—and bigger—fish to fry,' he said nastily with a sour glance Sebastian's way.

'He's just my boss, Mark.'

'Then why isn't he looking too pleased with your talking to another man?'

'Really?' Now it was Emily's turn to be shocked.

Actually, Sebastian did look a bit annoyed as he stepped up on to the pavement. By then, Mark had gone, like the coward that he was.

'Damned driver pretended he didn't have the right change,' Sebastian muttered as he joined her. 'In the end I gave him a fifty dollar note. Which I suppose was what he was angling for from the start. But I do resent giving large tips to people who do nothing for them.'

Emily castigated herself for entertaining the ridiculous notion that Sebastian could possibly be jealous. Her imagination was really working overtime today.

But that was becoming a habit whenever she was with Sebastian.

'This way,' he said, taking her arm and steering a safe path through the people hurrying to and fro.

Circular Quay was always busy, even on a Saturday, being a popular spot for tourists who flocked to see Sydney's most famous icons, its Harbour Bridge and Opera House, which admittedly were both unique and very beautiful.

Emily hadn't been in this part of the city for years, but she was familiar with the area. She had, after all, once been a working girl in the city. She'd lived with Mark in his apartment at Manly as well, catching the same ferry he caught every morning, just so she could spend every possible moment with him.

What a romantic fool she'd been back then!

Maybe she was still a romantic fool.

But not for much longer!

'So who was that man you were talking to just

now?' Sebastian asked as he guided her along the sun-drenched quay.

'And don't lie to me, Emily,' he went on before she could even open her mouth. 'I'm a good judge of body language and I know when a man and a woman have once meant something to each other. He couldn't take his eyes off you. And you...you looked almost murderous at running into him. If looks could kill...'

Emily supposed there was no reason not to tell him the truth. Though really her private life was none of his business.

'Mark's an old boyfriend,' she admitted.

'How old?'

'What do you mean?'

'How long ago did you break up?'

'About four years, give or take a month.'

'What happened?'

'My mother got cancer, that's what happened,' she said sharply, giving vent to some of the bitterness she'd bottled up for years. 'Mark didn't like my decision to go home and look after her. Prior to that, we were living together. But he couldn't cope with a girlfriend who wasn't there for him, twenty-four seven.'

'He obviously didn't care for you very deeply.'

'I did come to realise that,' Emily said with a sigh. 'But it was very hurtful to be dumped at such a distressing time.'

'You loved him a lot, didn't you?'

Emily wished she hadn't. But she had. And there was no point in denying it. 'Yes,' she said simply. 'I did.'

'He's the reason you haven't had a boyfriend since, isn't he?'

Emily began to feel uncomfortable with Sebastian pursuing this line of personal probing.

Grinding to a halt, she speared him with a firm look.

'Could we talk about something else, please?'

'I'm just trying to get to know you better,' he said.

'Why? So you'll know what buttons to push to persuade me to stay?'

He smiled a wry smile. 'You don't pull any punches, do you?'

'I just don't like being taken for a fool.'

'It would be very difficult to fool you, Emily.'

No, it wouldn't be, she thought as she glowered up at him. I've been made a fool of before. By Mark. And my father.

You could make a fool of me too. More easily than you know.

'I would hope that you wouldn't try,' she said in all seriousness.

He frowned, his eyes thoughtful. 'I would hope so too.'

'So what is this counter-offer you're going to make to me?' she asked, sick of not knowing. 'We're alone now, so there's no reason why you can't tell me.'

'I think we should get to the restaurant first,' he replied, 'before they give our booking to someone else.'

Emily smothered her irritation at yet another delay with some difficulty. Sebastian led her down to a nearby Thai restaurant which had an alfresco section outside that captured both the splendid view and the warm autumn sunshine. By the time they were settled at one of the brightly umbrellaed tables, and the drinks waiter had taken Sebastian's wine order, her patience was wearing very thin. Her stomach had begun churning with nervous anticipation, but her resolve to move on had grown stronger than ever.

'No more hedging, Sebastian,' she insisted. 'Out with it.'

'Very well,' he said, his piercing blue eyes locking with hers. 'I must warn you, however, that you'll probably be taken aback at first. Promise me that you will give my proposal due consideration. Don't reject it out of hand.'

'Your proposal of what?'

'Of marriage.'

Emily knew that if she'd been holding a glass of wine at that moment she would have dropped it, or spilt wine all over herself.

Taken aback did not begin to describe her reaction. Shocked was also inadequate. Stunned came close, but still fell short of capturing the emotions which crashed through her.

'In case I haven't made myself perfectly clear,' he swept on, 'I'm not proposing some kind of business arrangement, or a marriage in name only. This would be a real marriage in every sense of the word. I'm well aware you want at least one child, Emily, and I'm prepared to give you what you want.'

He couldn't be serious, she thought dazedly as she stared at him.

And yet he *was* serious!

She could see it in his eyes.

'I...I don't know what to say,' she choked out.

'Yes would be acceptable,' he replied with a small smile.

She stared at his smiling mouth, her own mouth still open and rapidly drying. She closed it and licked her parched lips, then shook her head, not in rejection, but in bewilderment.

'You don't propose marriage to your housekeeper, Sebastian, just to stop her from leaving. That's a crazy thing to do, especially for a man who's made it perfectly clear he never wanted to get married. Or become a father.'

She'd overheard him say as much to Lana. Loudly and firmly.

'I haven't up till now, that's true. But then I hadn't met a woman I wanted to marry. I want to marry you, Emily.'

'But *why?* You don't love me. You still love Lana. I know you do.'

'Then you know differently to me,' he stated quite coldly. 'I do not still love Lana. I never did.'

'Then why did you chase after her?'

He shrugged. 'There were things left unsaid which had to be said. My going to Italy was more a matter of curiosity. And closure.'

Emily was not in any way convinced. If that was the case, then why had he over-indulged in alcohol on the flight home? That was not like him at all. Sebastian liked a couple of glasses of wine with his meals, but she'd never seen him as intoxicated as he'd been last night.

He could say what he liked. He *had* loved Lana and he wasn't over her. Not by a long shot.

The drinks waiter arriving with the bottle of white wine Sebastian had ordered put paid to their conversation for a while, giving Emily the opportunity to get a grip on her emotions and think more rationally about Sebastian's marriage proposal.

It was utterly outrageous, of course.

But a very Sebastian thing to do.

In one fell swoop, he would solve both his current problems. Keep his housekeeper, plus fill the empty space Lana had left in his bed.

Thinking of filling Lana's space in his bed, however, sent Emily's head into a whirl. As much as she secretly thrilled to the prospect of Sebastian as her husband and lover, she could not discount the awful thought that if she married him she would always be a second-choice substitute for the woman he really wanted. What would happen when he got over his hurt and realised he'd married a woman who couldn't possibly fire up his passions the way Lana had? Would he want a divorce, or expect his wife of convenience to play the little woman at home whilst he took a mistress? Or two?

As much as Emily was madly tempted to still say yes, yes, yes and be damned with the consequences, her bitter experiences in the past kept warning her to stop and think. Did she really want to let herself be used by another man? Her father had used her, till her services were no longer required. Mark had done the same.

Could she rely on Sebastian being any different?

If anything, he might be worse, given his extreme wealth. Billionaires were used to getting their own way. Just because she thought the sun shone out of Sebastian didn't mean he didn't have a dark side. All men did.

By the time the drinks waiter left, Emily's head felt as if it would burst with the torment of her emotional dilemma.

For how could she possibly say no? She loved him and she wanted him.

It was the wanting which was the most difficult to resist. Last night she'd run from the chance of having Sebastian make love to her. How could she run from it again and not regret it till her dying day?

'Have a sip of the wine,' Sebastian suggested as soon as the drinks waiter left, 'and tell me what you think of it.'

Emily gripped her wineglass tightly lest her hand begin to shake. She brought it to her lips and sipped, then put it down carefully.

'Very nice,' she said.

'Have a guess where it comes from.'

Emily felt like throwing the wine in his arrogantly handsome face. But such overt tantrums weren't in her nature.

'New Zealand,' she answered. 'The Marlborough region.'

It was a game he played with her sometimes. Like most men, he liked to show off his own knowledge on a subject. But she knew her wines, her father having always kept an extensive cellar. Mark had been a wine buff as well so she'd had a very good schooling on the subject.

'Damn. I thought you might say Western Australia.'

'I've always liked New Zealand whites.'

'They do go well with Asian food. Have you decided what you're going to eat?' he added when another waiter materialised by their side, holding an order pad.

Emily had glanced at the menu sitting in front of her, but very blankly. Since Sebastian had dropped his bombshell, her mind had been on other things.

'Why don't you order for me?' she suggested, not really having much appetite. She was also beginning to feel quite warm, with her shoulders and arms in the sun.

Sebastian ordered a couple of noodle dishes, after which he stood up and took off his own suit jacket, draping it over the back of his chair.

Emily had seen him wearing a lot less. She already knew he had broad shoulders, a flat stomach and slim hips. So why did she have to stare at him the way she did?

Perhaps because she was already anticipating that moment when she would see him wearing absolutely nothing. Which she would, if she became his wife. He would be hers to look at. To kiss. To make love to.

The thought was mind-blowing. And a serious turn-on.

When his eyes met hers across the table, heat zoomed up her throat into her face.

'You should take your jacket off as well,' he said, thankfully misinterpreting the pink in her cheeks. 'You're looking hot.'

'Here,' he said, when she tried to struggle out of it whilst sitting down. 'Let me help you.'

She had to stand up, holding herself stiffly whilst he peeled the jacket back from her neck and lifted it up off her shoulders. Was she imagining it, or did he deliberately allow his fingertips to brush against her skin as he slid the jacket down her arms?

'I'll bet that feels better,' Sebastian remarked as he draped her jacket across the back of the chair next to her.

She sat down again and leant back in her chair, making a conscious effort to relax. Not an easy thing to do when her nipples were like bullets and her whole body was on the verge of spontaneous combustion.

She managed a small smile as he sat back down. 'It's turned out hotter today than I thought it would.'

His gaze flicked over her bare arms and shoulders, then back up to her face. His expression was guarded, his eyes unreadable. But the air between them crackled with an unspoken tension.

'Have you had enough time to think about my proposal?' he asked, his voice calm but his eyes watchful.

'Yes…'

'Good. Then what's it to be, Emily? Yes? Or no?'

Emily's head shouted no at her whilst her heart screamed yes.

At the last moment, she realised she didn't have

to say, either. Let him wait for her answer. And work a little harder for it.

'As I said earlier, Sebastian,' came her cool sounding reply. 'I don't like to rush my decisions. Could you give me the rest of the weekend to think about it?'

'The rest of the weekend,' he repeated slowly, looking not at all pleased by her answer.

'Yes. I'll let you know by Sunday night.'

'I would prefer to know where I stand today,' he ground out. 'Is there anything I could say, or do, to make up your mind a little earlier? Perhaps we could discuss your concerns over lunch, whatever they are.'

What a cold-blooded devil he was, Emily realised. No wonder Lana had left him. He had no idea how a woman felt. Or what a woman wanted.

Time to set him straight.

'The thing is, Sebastian, I always hoped that I would marry for love.'

'You loved your Mark,' he pointed out impatiently. 'If you'd married him, do you think you would have been happy?'

'Perhaps not.'

'Love as a basis for marriage is seriously over-rated,' he argued. 'Just look at the divorce rate in the Western world where most marriages are love matches. Caring, compatibility and commitment are much better bets.'

'But what if we're *not* compatible?'

'But we already are,' he said. 'We get along very well together, Emily. Surely you can see that.'

'In a platonic fashion. But what about sexually?'

Her question startled him, his brows drawing together in an almost affronted fashion. 'You think I can't satisfy you in bed?'

'I don't know. That's the point. I would never marry a man who was inadequate in the bedroom,' she answered with a superbly straight face. 'For all his flaws, Mark was an excellent lover.'

He stared at her long and hard across the table till she wished she hadn't dared challenge him in such a silly fashion. He was not a man you threw down the gauntlet to.

But perhaps that was why she'd done it. Because subconsciously she knew he'd pick it up.

'If that is your main concern,' he said, his eyes clashing boldly with hers, 'it can be easily dispensed with. Spend tonight with me. Find out for yourself what kind of lover I am.'

Emily stopped her mouth from gaping open this time, her pride demanding she not betray herself by suddenly acting like some love-struck fool. Though possibly she was more lust-struck at that moment.

'You're very sure of yourself, aren't you?' she said with deceptive calm. If he could see her insides, he'd know the truth.

'I know what I'm good at.'

'But what about me? What if you find out *I'm* hopeless in the bedroom?'

His eyes searched her face. '*Are* you?'

'I guess that depends,' she said, 'on whom I'm with.'

'You like to be in love with your lovers?'

'I like to believe they love me.'

'Love and great sex do not have to go together, Emily. I could prove that to you tonight.'

No, you won't, she thought despairingly. Because I already love you. Having you make love to me is going to feel great, no matter what you do.

'I...I'll think about it,' came her slightly shaky answer.

Suddenly she couldn't bear to sit there any longer. She had to get away from him for a while. Had to have a few moments to herself.

'If you'll excuse me, Sebastian,' she said, putting down her glass and scooping up her handbag from the adjacent chair, 'I need to go to the ladies'.'

CHAPTER SIX

SEBASTIAN watched Emily flee the table. And him.

Not that she ran. She walked. But he could see flight in her body language.

Things were not going as he'd anticipated.

He had expected her to be surprised by his marriage proposal. But he'd also expected her to say yes, once it sank in what marriage to him would give her.

A beautiful home she'd always admired. A husband who liked and respected her. Plus a lifestyle which would make her the envy of every woman in Australia.

What more could a girl like Emily want?

He was even prepared to give her a child.

And what had she focused on?

Love. And then sex.

That had seriously surprised him. When his practical and pragmatic housekeeper had outlined her husband-hunting plans this morning, she hadn't mentioned craving love and sex. Just a husband and a child before she got too old.

Sebastian had never imagined for one moment that Emily was a closet romantic.

His right hand reached into his jacket pocket, his fingers wrapping around the box which contained the very expensive engagement ring he'd bought this morning.

For a moment he contemplated taking it out and presenting her with it on her return. There was something about a huge diamond which usually melted a woman's resistance.

Unfortunately, Emily was not a usual woman.

She was different from every other woman he'd ever known. Right from the first moment he'd met her, he'd recognised that she was unique, projecting an air of capability and maturity far beyond her years. No wonder he'd believed she was older than she really was.

Within no time she'd brought an organised and peaceful atmosphere to his home which he'd come to rely on.

No, not just rely on. Which he needed.

He needed Emily in his life, a lot more than he'd ever needed Lana. When Lana had left, he'd been angry and frustrated. Sebastian was a possessive man who didn't like to let go, or to lose. But his drinking too much on the flight home yesterday had not been the result of a broken heart but a case of self disgust. The only good thing to come out of his chasing after Lana was finding out he never wanted to see her ever again.

When Emily had announced she was leaving him, however, Sebastian had known within seconds of reading her resignation letter that he would do anything to keep her. Anything at all!

When the idea of marriage had first popped into his mind he'd honestly believed he'd come up with the perfect solution. What woman in her right mind would say no to the most eligible bachelor in Australia?

Emily Bayliss, that was who.

So much for Lana snidely remarking one day that his housekeeper had a crush on him. She couldn't have been further from the truth.

Which left Sebastian no alternative but to move on to Plan B.

The only problem was he hadn't worked out what Plan B was as yet.

But he would think of something.

He'd be ruthless if he had to be.

By the time Emily emerged from the ladies' room, she had come to a decision.

It was a very bold decision, and one which left her quaking inside. But she simply could not go to her grave regretting that she'd knocked back the chance to go to bed with the man she loved.

So she would accept Sebastian's offer to spend the night with him.

But she would not marry him.

Of course she would not tell him that in advance, otherwise he might retract the offer of sex. She would let him think her saying yes to his suggestion was likely to lead to her saying yes to his proposal.

Emily could only hope and pray that when the

morning came she would have the courage to say no and walk away.

Because to marry Sebastian would be setting herself up for future misery and heartache. And she'd had enough of that in her lifetime already. She wanted a marriage which would bring her peace and contentment, not emotional turmoil.

No doubt Sebastian could provide her with every material comfort, and possibly a great amount of physical comfort. But no comfort for her already damaged heart and her long-suffering soul.

Their meals had arrived, she noted as she returned to the table, which was good. She could talk about the food, thereby hiding her growing tension.

'This smells delicious,' she said as she sat down quickly and picked up her fork.

'They're called drunken noodles,' he informed her, then smiled. 'I thought it was an appropriate choice, given my appalling state last night.'

Emily might have relaxed at this point if she hadn't known what was ahead of her.

One part of her wanted to get it over and done with, that terrifying moment when she'd have to look him in the eyes and say, *By the way, Sebastian, I think it's a good idea, our going to bed together tonight.*

But she simply could not find her tongue, her eyes dropping to her food.

'You know, Emily, you have a very beautiful body.'

Her eyes jerked upwards at his softly delivered words.

No, not softly. Seductively. As seductive as his eyes which were travelling slowly over her body now, implying that his offer to sleep with her was not just to prove a point but because he desired her.

Her mouth dried as her heart thudded within her chest.

'Thank you,' she choked out.

'You are a very beautiful woman all round,' he went on mercilessly. 'Please don't think I asked you to marry me just because I wanted you to stay on as my housekeeper. I'll hire another housekeeper, if and when you marry me.'

'But I wouldn't like that,' she blurted out before she could think better of it.

'You prefer to take care of me and my home yourself?'

'No...Yes...I mean...'

'You can do whatever you want, Emily,' he inter-rupted in that soft, silky voice. '*Have* whatever you want. I am a very wealthy man, as you know.'

Suddenly she saw what he was doing. He was trying to seduce her. And corrupt her.

Emily knew exactly what Sebastian wanted. For the status quo in his household to stay the same, even if he had to give her the title of wife, plus give her a bit of something else as well.

Emily could not help feeling cynical about all of Sebastian's proposals. And about the so-called desire she'd seen in his eyes just now.

Let's face it, girl, she told herself. He hadn't wanted to marry you before today, had he?

'I think we're getting ahead of ourselves,' she said firmly. 'I won't be rushed into something as serious as marriage, Sebastian. But I do think your idea of our spending tonight together is a sensible one.'

His eyes widened slightly at her cool acceptance of his sexual proposal.

For a long moment he stared at her, his gaze thoughtful and probing. But she held her ground, and her outer composure.

It was just as well, however, that he could not see her inner turmoil.

Or was it excitement making her heart race and her stomach churn?

'I trust you haven't changed your mind about that,' she added in a challenging tone.

The hint of a smile pulled at the corners of his mouth. 'Absolutely not.'

'That's good, then,' she said matter-of-factly. 'Now, I think we should get on with our drunken noodles before they get cold.'

Emily fell to eating with apparent gusto. But in fact she had to force every mouthful down. A lump seemed to have lodged in her throat.

Whenever she stopped to take a gulp of wine, Sebastian glanced up from his meal to gaze at her with those far too intelligent eyes of his.

What was he thinking? she kept wondering, and worrying.

As much as Sebastian tried, he could not quite grasp what was going on in Emily's head.

But he had to admire her. What other woman would react as Emily had today?

Her lack of enthusiasm for his marriage proposal, then her amazingly cool agreement to spending tonight with him had certainly put him on the back foot, a position which he did not like.

Sebastian enjoyed being the boss. At work, at home and in the bedroom. *Especially* in the bedroom.

Time to take the reins again.

'Mountains or the ocean?' he asked when she next reached for her wineglass.

Her glass froze in mid-air, her expression confused. 'What?'

Sebastian picked up his own glass and took a leisurely swallow.

'Which do you prefer?' he asked smoothly. 'The mountains or the ocean?'

'Um… The ocean.'

'Then the ocean it is.'

'I have no idea what you're talking about.'

'Where we will spend tonight. I'll find us a nice hotel on the south coast. Which means I won't be able to drink too much more of this wine. Not if I have to drive. You can have my share.'

'But…do we *have* to go away? Why can't we just stay home?'

'Come now, Emily, I wouldn't expect you to share the bed I shared with Lana.' He'd noticed this morning that it still smelt of Lana's perfume, a powerfully exotic scent which seemed to have seeped into the mattress. Maybe even the carpet as well.

Now that Lana was definitely out of the picture, Sebastian planned on having the whole room refurbished. He wanted nothing left to remind him of that bitch.

'But I...I don't have any nice clothes for going away,' Emily protested. 'Other than what I have on.'

'Which will be highly suitable for arriving and leaving in,' he said. 'Between those times, you won't be needing many clothes.'

At last he got the reaction he wanted.

Heat zoomed into her cheeks, giving him a glimpse of the woman she might become in his arms.

His own body responded, reminding him of the way he'd felt last night, when he'd watched her swimming naked in his pool. *Before* he'd known it was Emily. He'd been transfixed by her voluptuous body...and turned on to the max.

Tonight, that same highly detectable body would be his to make love to.

It was a tantalising and very arousing thought.

Sebastian had deliberately kept his proposal of marriage very businesslike, because that was what he'd believed would appeal to Emily. But there'd been several moments already today when he'd been tempted to cast aside pragmatism in favour of the caveman approach.

When she'd shown up for lunch looking absolutely gorgeous, he'd wanted to do more than take her elbow. He'd wanted to pull her into his arms and kiss her till she was incapable of saying anything but yes to whatever he wanted, whenever he wanted it.

Then, in the taxi, he'd found it extremely hard to keep his hands to himself with her sitting so close to him. Only the fact that they were not alone had stopped him from pouncing.

Tonight, however, they would be alone, with no one to stop him.

Yet his mission was not to satisfy his own, surprisingly intense desires, he reminded himself. But to give Emily the night of her life.

Sebastian had no idea what she liked, sexually. But he knew what just about every woman in the world liked.

Romance.

He intended to give her that. In spades.

CHAPTER SEVEN

'WHAT on earth have you done?' Emily asked the flushed face in her bathroom mirror.

She kept shaking her head at herself, all her earlier boldness nothing but a dim memory.

The rest of their lunch had passed in a bit of a haze, as had their taxi ride home. She hadn't spoken much. But then, neither had Sebastian. Not till they'd emerged from the taxi.

'Give me some time to organise things,' he'd said as he'd walked her up to the house. 'It's just gone three. I'll come and collect you around four. Like I said, don't pack a lot. A change of underwear and some toiletries. Maybe something casual, in case we go for a walk at some stage.'

Emily had managed to appear as cool as Sebastian till she'd reached the privacy of her apartment, at which point she'd rushed to the bathroom for a desperate call of nature.

Now here she was, on the verge of tears.

Till she suddenly thought of Mark. Then her father.

Would they cry in her situation?

Never in a million years!

If Mark had been a woman, he'd have been jubilant. Though, come to think of it, he wouldn't have been in her situation, because he'd have agreed to marry Sebastian like a shot.

Money was Mark's god.

Emily wished she could think more like a man. They could separate love and sex so very easily. They compartmentalised.

Emily couldn't do that, although she was quite adept at hiding her feelings. When she'd been nursing her terminally ill mother, she'd become an expert at the brave face, and on putting a positive spin on the most depressing reality.

Thinking about her mother's death brought some perspective to Emily's thinking. Her situation with Sebastian, whilst upsetting, was hardly tragic. At least she was getting the opportunity to have the man she loved make love to her. How bad could that be?

Emily held on to this new, more positive attitude whilst she went and packed, as ordered. A change of underwear and toiletries were no problem. Choosing a casual outfit proved a little more difficult, because there wasn't much to choose from in her 'house-keeper' wardrobe.

She finally selected a pair of stretch jeans which she'd only worn when Sebastian had been away, a simple white T-shirt, a dark blue jacket and a pair of black shoes.

Her packing complete, Emily stripped off and had

a quick shower, careful not to mess up her hair. Afterwards, she swiftly reapplied her make-up, then sprayed herself all over with the only perfume she owned, a light flowery scent which her mother had always worn and which brought fond memories of the hugs they'd shared.

It was nothing like the heavy musky scent Lana had practically bathed in. But then, she was nothing like Lana, except perhaps in bust size.

Lana had been a curvy girl too.

But not quite as curvy as me, Emily thought with secret satisfaction. She had not forgotten how Sebastian had stared at her bare breasts in the pool last night. Not with disgust. With desire.

What will it be like tonight, she wondered, when he saw her again without any clothes on? How would it feel when he touched her? Kissed her? Entered her?

A low moan escaped her lips at this last thought, her hands shaking as she stepped into her cream satin bikini pants.

This was why she'd made the bold decision she had, Emily accepted anew as she dragged on her panties, and then the rest of her clothes. Because she simply had to be with this man. It was a craving which would not be denied.

Once dressed, Emily came to another bold decision. She would not worry about the morning-after any more, would not stew over the consequences of tonight.

For the rest of today, she was going to compartmentalise her thoughts, blotting out all female emotions and focusing on one thing and one thing only.

The pleasure of the moment.

Looking at her completed appearance in the mirror gave her pleasure. Thinking of tonight as an exciting adventure, rather than being fearful of it, sent extremely pleasurable quivers rippling all through her.

If this was what a man's thinking was like, Emily decided, it was much better than a woman's. She vowed to keep it up for as long as she could.

The doorbell ringing two minutes later rattled her resolve momentarily. But then she squared her shoulders, picked up her overnight bag and went to answer the door.

'Oh!' she exclaimed when she opened it and saw Sebastian standing there. 'You've changed your clothes.'

'Only partially,' he replied as he took the bag out of her hands. 'The suit's the same. Just the shirt and tie have gone.'

They certainly had, replaced by a sexy black crew neck top.

Emily had always thought Sebastian a handsome man. But she'd never thought him over-whelmingly sexy till she'd realised she'd fallen in love with him. It was as though, with this discovery, her eyes finally saw what her heart had sub-consciously seen from the word go. That her boss possessed a physical magnetism which was totally irresistible.

To her, anyway.

Her blood charged around her veins as her gaze

travelled over him from top to toe. What a stunningly sexy man he was. And tonight he was hers, as she was all his.

Emily could not wait to give herself to him. But not as some kind of sacrificial lamb. Tonight she would take as well as give, without the emotional turmoil which a one-sided love might have brought to their lovemaking.

'Have you got everything you want in here?' Sebastian asked, nodding down to the bag in his hands.

'I hope so.'

'Let's go, then.'

'I have to get my handbag.'

'I'll walk down and put this in the car. You lock up and meet me in the garage.'

A minute later Emily was running down the stairs, her pulse rate as excited as she was. She told herself to slow down and not start acting like a giddy schoolgirl on her first date.

But that was exactly what she felt like.

But then Sebastian wouldn't date schoolgirls.

Sebastian was standing by the passenger door of his magnificent silver sports car in the garage, his face breaking into a smile when she hurried in.

'You're my kind of girl, Emily,' he said as he opened the passenger door and waved her inside. 'You don't keep a man waiting.'

Lana had, Emily recalled, as she lowered herself into the leather bucket seat. All the time.

Emily frowned. Darn. She hadn't wanted to think about Lana.

Still, he hadn't asked Lana to marry him, had he, came the reassuring thought.

When Sebastian closed the passenger door after her, Emily's nostrils were immediately assailed with the smell of new leather. The car was only a couple of months old, Sebastian's previous vehicle of choice having been a more sedate BMW.

'I like the smell of new cars,' she remarked when Sebastian climbed in behind the wheel.

'You sound like you've got a lot of experience,' he said as he fired the powerful engine.

Emily shrugged. 'My father's always trading in his car and getting a new one.'

Sebastian glanced over at her with curious eyes. 'You've never spoken of your father before.'

'He's not exactly my favourite person,' came her clipped reply.

Sebastian's eyebrows rose. 'I suspect he might be a subject best left to another day.'

'I suspect you could be right.'

'In that case I will keep our conversation to more pleasant topics.'

'Please do.'

Sebastian stopped talking long enough to back out of the garage, swinging his car sharply right once they had cleared the door. It closed automatically, after which Sebastian reefed the wheel to the left and accelerated up the driveway. The large security gates forced a stop, though Sebastian didn't have to get out to open them. He had a remote control which he always carried with him.

Emily had one too, which she kept in the glove box of her car.

'You smell very nice,' he said whilst they sat there, waiting for the gates to open wide enough to drive through.

Emily's initial reaction to his compliment was negative. Because she didn't think it could be sincere. Clearly, Sebastian would have liked Lana's heavier perfume, and her own was very light by comparison.

But she swiftly pushed aside such thoughts. Today was for positive thoughts, not negative.

'You do too,' she returned with a smile.

Her own compliment startled him. But then he smiled as well, a wickedly sexy smile, which sent a tremor running down Emily's spine.

The gates finally open, Sebastian zoomed through, not waiting till they were fully shut behind them before he turned left and sped up the tree-lined avenue.

'Where, exactly, are we going?' she asked at the first set of lights.

'North Wollongong. To the Norfolk. It's a newish hotel right on the beach. I stayed there last year.'

Emily winced. Not with Lana, she hoped.

'No,' he said straight away. 'Not with Lana.'

Her head whipped around. 'How did you know what I was thinking?'

'I know how women's minds work.'

Emily could imagine that he did, given he must have had relationships with dozens of women during his adult life. Being such a perfectionist, he would have learned all he could about the female psyche, along with their bodies. Clearly, he had no doubts or worries about his performance tonight.

Still, Emily found Sebastian's sexual confidence a turn-on.

Not that she needed a turn-on where Sebastian was concerned. He only had to be in the same room with her these days and she was turned on.

Being in the same car with him, especially such a sexy one, was doing things to her that were positively indecent. She could hardly sit still in her leather seat.

No wonder men of the world always drove sports cars, Emily decided with a mixture of admiration and cynicism. They made foreplay almost unnecessary. She suspected that by the time they arrived at that hotel on the south coast she would be in a seriously excited state.

Emily had always liked sex. Mark had not been her first lover, by any means. But she had never craved it as she craved it at this moment. Had never wanted the kinds of things she was suddenly wanting with Sebastian.

She hoped he would not be gentle with her. Or sweet. Or, heaven forbid, loving. She wanted it rough, and wild.

The first time.

After that, she wanted it slow and sensual, so that she could wallow in the experience. Finally, she wanted the opportunity to give, rather than receive. She could see herself now, stroking him all over, kissing him all over, forcing him to lie back whilst she made mad passionate love to him.

Emily's heartbeat took off at the images which flooded into her mind.

'You're very quiet,' Sebastian said. 'You don't get car sick, do you?'

Emily swallowed, taking a moment to clear the breathtakingly exciting fantasy from her mind.

'Not usually. But you do drive fast, Sebastian,' she added as he zipped around a corner and down a narrow side street.

To be honest, Emily had no idea where she was. She never did in Sydney if she didn't stick to the main roads. Which Sebastian obviously hadn't.

'I'm an impatient person by nature,' he replied.

'Really? I wouldn't have said you were.'

'Most people wouldn't. But I am. I just hide my flaws better than most. I'm very impatient, and inclined to lose my temper far too quickly.'

'You never have with me.'

'No one could lose their temper with you, Emily.'

Emily wasn't so sure that was a compliment. It made her sound very boring. And lacking in passion.

'Unlike Lana, you mean,' she couldn't help saying.

'Lana who?' he quipped.

'Oh, I see,' she said. 'So that's how it is with you, is it? Once out of your life, a person doesn't exist any more.'

'That's right.'

Emily shook her head. 'I wish I could do that.' As much as she tried to hate her father, she knew she didn't. She still loved him. And whilst she didn't love Mark any more, she would never forget him, or the callously insensitive way he'd treated her.

'It takes practice,' Sebastian said so coldly that it sent a shiver down Emily's spine.

How bitter he sounded. And ruthless.

It was at that point she realised how little she actually knew about Sebastian. Oh, she'd read the articles about his brilliant business acumen, and seen a short segment on TV outlining how his career had got started; how he and a friend had started up one of the first Australian mobile phone companies when they'd been in their early twenties. Sebastian had had the brains and his wealthy friend had provided the backing, Sebastian revealing during that programme that, unlike his rich business partner, he'd had to work his way through university, his family being very working-class.

Both young men had made an absolute fortune when their chain of Mobilemania stores had been bought out by an international conglomerate. His friend had disappeared from the business scene after that. But Sebastian had started up his own company, Armstrong Industries, developing a wide range of business interests, from holiday resorts to day-care centres to cattle stations and even pine forests.

Sebastian had made the Richest Two Hundred in Australia list by the time he'd been thirty. Recently he'd made the top ten, one of only a select number of billionaires.

The public at large knew about his bank balance,

and his single status. But what did they really know—Emily included—about his background?

Very little.

Maybe the media would have dug deeper if he'd been the kind of man who sought publicity.

But he didn't. He kept a very low media profile for a man of his wealth and power.

Emily did know he'd been an only child, courtesy of a remark he'd made during her initial interview when she'd said she was was one too. But she knew nothing of his parents, or his extended family, except that they never visited him.

Presumably his parents were dead.

Although curious, Emily was not about to ask.

Because today was about the pleasure of the moment, not bringing up awkward subjects.

'Now I know where I am!' she exclaimed when Sebastian finally directed his car out on to a main road. 'That's the Olympic stadium over there.'

'Did you go to the Olympics?' Sebastian asked.

'No. I wanted to, but my boyfriend at the time wasn't into sport.'

'Are you talking about that Mark fellow?'

'Er...no. The one before him.'

His eyes speared her for a brief but intense moment. 'You're not the quiet little mouse you've been pretending to be, are you?'

'I haven't been pretending anything,' she said defensively. 'I simply needed to withdraw from relationships for a while.'

'And now you're ready to go back into them?'

'Yes.'

'Complete with a new look.'

'Well I wasn't about to snare myself a husband looking the way I did, was I?'

'I don't know about that. You captured my interest.'

'Oh, don't be ridiculous, Sebastian. You hardly recognised me as a woman till you saw me in my birthday suit.'

'You'd be wrong there. But you did change my perspective on your personality when I found you skinny-dipping in my pool.'

'You didn't think I had it in me?'

'I thought it was out of character.'

'Well. Just shows you that you don't know everything. Even if you think you do,' she added saucily.

He laughed. 'You delight me, Emily.'

'I'm not trying to.'

'I know. That's what delights me. Do you have any idea what most women would do, if they were in your circumstances today?'

'I can guess. But I have a different agenda to most women.'

'Would you care to elaborate?'

'No.'

'Damn it, Emily, I might be tempted to lose my temper with you after all!'

'Won't do you any good.'

'No,' he sighed. 'I dare say it wouldn't. You wouldn't want to marry a man who yelled at you.'

'Absolutely not. And I wouldn't want to marry a man I didn't know, either. When I marry, I want to feel secure in my choice. I don't want any nasty surprises.'

'But you *do* know me. Hell, Emily, you've been my housekeeper for eighteen months. You've seen me in all sorts of situations and moods. More importantly, I haven't been trying to impress you, or hide things from you. My life is an open book. How long do you think it'll take you to get to know whatever new man you're going to meet at that conference centre? Years, if you want to know everything about him. By the time you feel secure enough to marry, your biological clock will be well and truly at midnight. And a baby is what you want more than anything, isn't it?'

Emily's heart lurched. What she wanted more than anything was his baby! To go along with his love…One without the other would be too bitter-sweet for her.

'Agree to marry me,' he swept on before she'd answered him. 'And we could start on the baby-making project tonight.'

Emily gasped, her head snapping round to stare at him.

'You are a truly wicked man, Sebastian Armstrong.'

'A determined man, Emily Bayliss. So what do you say?'

'I'm positively speechless.'

'That's a cop-out. Tell me what you're thinking.'

'I'm thinking I made a big mistake being here with you,' she snapped. 'I should have known you'd know exactly what buttons to push to try to force my hand and get your own way. You're a clever man, Sebastian. But a far too cold-blooded one. I wouldn't want such a man as the father of my children.'

CHAPTER EIGHT

EMILY'S vehement criticism of his character stunned Sebastian.

He'd honestly thought she liked and respected him.

His shock swiftly gave way to angry frustration. What was the point in going on if that was the way she felt? Clearly, she wasn't about to say yes to his proposal of marriage, no matter how good a lover he was.

Sebastian came to a quick decision, zapping his car around the next corner, before braking to a sharp stop at the kerb.

'It's very easy to fix your big mistake, Emily,' he ground out as he glared over at her startled face. 'I'll take you back home.'

Her expressive eyes betrayed an intriguing truth. She didn't want him to take her home.

Which meant only one thing.

She might think he was a total bastard. But she still wanted him to take her to bed.

Sebastian's eyebrows arched. Maybe he wasn't

the only one in this car who was a bit on the cold-blooded side.

Still, he understood full well the perversities of sexual attraction. He'd wanted Lana from the first moment he'd seen her. Had wanted her, despite knowing she was a vain, shallow, temperamental creature of whom instinct warned he should steer well clear.

It was damned hard to act sensibly when your hormones were up and running.

'You don't want me to take you home,' he stated baldly, and watched her reaction.

She looked away, as a lot of women did when they were faced with an unpalatable fact.

'There's nothing wrong with wanting sex, Emily,' he argued. 'From what you've told me, you've been without a man for four years. That's not natural, not for a woman who's had an active sex life, which I gather you did have, once. Look, we'll forget about marriage and babies for tonight and just have a good time together.'

Slowly, very slowly, her head turned back. Sebastian was taken aback to see that her eyes were glistening.

Her distress upset him, far more than Lana's copious tears and tantrums ever had. This was no cold-blooded creature sitting next to him, he realised, but a deeply feeling, highly sensitive woman.

Her eyes dropped to her lap as she shook her head unhappily from side to side.

'I won't let you run away from your feelings,

Emily,' he persisted. 'You might not like me, but you need me.'

Her head jerked up and round to glare at him. '*Need* you? I don't *need* you,' she threw at him as she dashed her tears away with the back of her hands.

'Yes, you do. Well, maybe not me, especially. But you need a man. Someone who can get rid of that build-up of sexual frustration you're obviously suffering from. Someone who can show you that you don't need love to enjoy sex.'

'You have absolutely *no* hope of doing *that*, Sebastian.'

Sebastian was not a man to take a challenge lightly.

'Really,' he grated out. And, before she could do more than blink at him, he leant over and kissed her.

When Sebastian's lips crashed down on hers, Emily tried not to moan. Or to melt. Or, heaven forbid, open her own instantly treacherous mouth.

But it was like offering a starving woman a delicious dish of food and expecting her only to have a tiny taste.

So she moaned… And melted… And opened her mouth…

And it all felt fantastic. His lips, his tongue, his hand curving possessively around her throat, pushing her back against the leather seat, holding her captive.

How passionate he was, she thought with an almost delirious joy. How masterful. Exactly as she'd imagined in her fantasies.

When the pressure on her mouth eased, Emily's

left hand instinctively lifted to cup the back of his head and keep the kiss going. She didn't want him to stop. Ever.

Sebastian groaned as he battled to gain control of himself.

Who would believe that kissing Emily would do this to him?

If he didn't stop kissing her soon, he'd be forced to do something he hadn't done in years. Have sex in the front seat of a car. In broad daylight.

This was not what he'd planned.

Still, nothing had gone as he'd planned.

If only she'd stop making those sexy little noises—stop squirming…stop digging her nails into him.

Hell on earth, he was dying to touch her, as well as kiss her. She wanted him to. He could tell.

But if he did…

Sebastian reminded himself of what was waiting for them at that hotel: a luxury suite, a king-sized bed, champagne on ice, chocolate-dipped strawberries and candles around the spa bath.

He'd left no stone unturned in providing the most romantic atmosphere for tonight, his mission not just to seduce Emily sexually, but to put her in the right frame of mind to accept his proposal.

If he went ahead with what he was doing right at this moment, she wouldn't be impressed afterwards. She'd be disgusted with herself, and with him. He'd hardly get her to change her mind about his character—and his offer of marriage—if he took cruel advantage of her sexual frustration.

With Emily clearly in desperate need of some lovemaking, Sebastian's goal of making her his wife was back on the agenda, no longer a mission impossible but a definite possibility. By her own admission, Emily was the type of girl who had difficulty separating sex and love. If he satisfied her in bed, she might surrender her heart to him, as well as her body.

This last thought held a lot of appeal. A woman in love was often willing to do things which her head warned her against.

No, he had to stop. And he had to stop right now!

No, don't stop, Emily screamed silently when Sebastian wrenched his mouth away.

He removed her hand—the one which was still caressing the back of his head—and pressed it forcibly down into her lap.

'This is not the place for this, Emily,' he ground out. 'Not nearly enough room. But no more nonsense now. I'm driving us down to that hotel and you're not going to say a single word the whole way. Conversation with you, I can see, is a risk. So zip that lovely mouth of yours up and keep it for what it does very well indeed. And no, I don't want any more of those shock-horror looks either. We both know you came with me today to be kissed, and a whole lot more.'

Emily opened her mouth to voice some kind of lame protest. But closed it again when he pressed two fingers against her lips, his eyes filling with a dark warning.

'Speak, and I promise you I will make you do things in this car which will truly horrify you afterwards.'

Emily almost laughed. Dear heaven, if only he knew...

Her lips parted slightly against the flesh of his fingers, her heart pounding within her chest. Her earlier qualms about coming with Sebastian today had been well and truly routed with his hungry kisses, all doubts replaced by a desire so intense she wasn't sure she could bear any more delay.

'I'll put the radio on,' he said, abruptly withdrawing his hand and doing just that, the car filling with music, a popular song about love lost.

'I suggest you lie back and get some rest,' he said as he gunned the engine once more. 'Because you're going to be damned busy from the moment we reach the privacy of our room.'

A highly erotic quiver rippled through Emily. She'd always known Sebastian would be a passionate lover. And an imaginative one. When Lana had stayed over, she'd always come down to the breakfast table smiling like a cat who'd got the cream.

Her heart suddenly squeezed tight behind her ribs, her eyes darting over to Sebastian, who was busy doing a U-turn.

Is he really over that woman? she agonised. Or will he be thinking of her whilst he's making love to me? Comparing us, perhaps.

'We'll soon be on the freeway,' Sebastian told her as he rejoined the traffic on the main road. 'We should be pulling up at the hotel in just over an hour. Now close your eyes,' he ordered. 'And relax.'

His telling her to relax reinforced to Emily just

how different men were from women. Maybe he could relax after what had just happened. But she found it almost impossible.

Still, it came to her that he probably wasn't thinking of Lana at all. She was being ridiculously insecure and jealous.

Men lived in and for the moment, which was what she was supposed to be doing today. Living for the pleasure of the moment and not worrying about anything else, especially Lana.

Which was fine in theory, Emily had come to realise. Not so easy in practice. For her, anyway.

It was as well that Sebastian had taken command of the situation. Because he'd been so right. She hadn't wanted him to take her home. She wanted to have this one night to remember for the rest of her life.

For Sebastian, it would just be a night of no-strings sex, the kind men obviously enjoyed. For her, it would probably prove to be a bitter-sweet experience. But one which she would never regret.

If the effect of his kisses was anything to go by, she was going to have a fabulous time, sexually. Her whole body quivered just thinking about it.

Of course, the morning after was going to be difficult.

Despite what he'd said, Emily was not convinced that Sebastian had given up his quest to stop her from leaving him. He was an extremely stubborn man, and a super rich one, grown used to having his way.

She wouldn't mind betting he still thought he could seduce her into doing what he wanted.

Emily could not deny that when he was kissing her just now, all sensible thought had flown out the window. But he couldn't make love to her all the time. She would have some moments of respite, such as now.

Finally, Emily closed her eyes, leant back in the seat and focused on some sensible survival mantras.

Don't forget he doesn't love you, no matter what his lovemaking is like.

Don't forget he's only taking you to bed to get his own way.

Don't forget it's just sex to him. Nothing more.

CHAPTER NINE

EMILY couldn't really relax, of course. She just pretended to so that Sebastian would leave her alone. After a while, she turned her head and shoulders to face the passenger window so that he couldn't see when she opened her eyes.

By then, they were on the freeway. The southern Sydney suburbs had been left behind and they were speeding along the multi-lane highway which cut its path through national forests.

Thick bushland edged the road on either side.

Not the most distracting of views.

Emily hadn't been down to the south coast in years. She and Mark had always headed north when they'd wanted to go somewhere for the day, or a weekend. But she'd had a boyfriend once who lived in Campbelltown, and he'd often taken her down to Austinmere, a cute little beach on the south coast which had a sea pool. He'd also taken her to Thirlmere, which was more of a surfer's beach. She'd never actually been to Wollongong, which was the largest of the south coast towns. A city, really.

Once they were on the freeway, there were two ways of reaching their destination. You could get off the highway and go down the Bulli Pass, then follow the road south along the coastline to North Wollongong.

That was considered the tourist route, providing spectacular views.

The Bulli pass, however, was a formidable descent, with lots of hairpin bends.

Alternately, you could keep on the Princes Highway till you reached Wollongong proper. This was a faster route, with a more gradual descent from the hills to the coast, but less interesting.

When the sign for the Bulli Pass exit came up, Sebastian stayed in the centre lane, clearly going for the faster route. Fifteen minutes later, the bushland receded and Wollongong came into view below.

Emily actually spotted their hotel as they made their way down the escarpment, the tall white building standing out from its surroundings, the last rays of the setting sun just catching the upper floor windows. But she didn't realise it was the Norfolk till Sebastian turned his car into the circular driveway which led up to its equally impressive entrance.

'Wow,' Emily said, sitting upright in her seat. It was the first word she'd spoken since Sebastian had ordered her not to.

His sidewards glance carried a self-satisfied smile. 'You approve?'

'It's stunning.' And very expensive, by the look of it.

Emily knew her hotels. And this one would rival the very best in Sydney.

A parking valet pounced immediately they alighted, as well as a porter to take their two small bags. Sebastian cupped her elbow and led her through the revolving glass doors into the hotel proper, Emily doing her best to act as if this was what she did most weekends—stayed in five-star hotels with one of Australia's wealthiest and most eligible men.

The lobby was enormous, with marble floors, vaulted ceilings and some serious chandeliers which would not have looked out of place in a European palace.

The blonde behind the reception desk nearly fell over herself attending to Sebastian, Emily mentally shaking her head over the girl's gushing manner. During the time she'd worked the desk at the Regency, they'd had presidents, pop stars and even a sheikh or two staying there and she hadn't gone gaga over any of them.

The blonde even had the hide to cast an askance glance Emily's way when Sebastian was busy signing in, as though she could not understand what on earth he was doing with such an ordinary-looking girlfriend.

Emily squared her shoulders and speared the receptionist with dagger-like eyes until the girl flushed and looked away. By the time Sebastian led Emily over to the lift wells, she had her dander up, which was much better than succumbing to the butterflies gathering in the pit of her stomach.

'Do women always act like that when you're around?' she asked when he let go of her arm to press the up button on the wall.

His shrug was dismissive. 'In the main.'

'No wonder you're arrogant.'

Sebastian's eyes turned dark and thoughtful. 'Are you deliberately trying to provoke me, Emily?'

Was she?

Guilt consumed Emily once she realised she'd been trying to sabotage tonight one last time. Possibly because of fear.

'I'm sorry,' she said. 'That was rude of me.'

'Yes, it was.'

'I'm not usually rude.'

'I know. So why were you just now?'

'I guess it's because I'm nervous,' she confessed.

'Nervous?' he repeated, as though unfamiliar with such a condition.

'It's so silly,' she blurted out. 'It's not as though I'm a virgin.'

'Maybe not,' he said, his eyes soft on her. 'But it will be your first time in a long time. And your first time with me.'

'Yes,' she whispered through parched lips.

The lift doors opened and a couple came out, putting a stop to their intimate conversation. But not to Emily's rapidly escalating heartbeat.

When Sebastian took hold of her hand an electric

current raced up her arm. Apprehension gave way to anticipation, doubt replaced by the most overwhelming need, not to be made love to, but to be totally ravished. Her head turned and her eyes locked with his.

'Don't be gentle with me,' she heard herself say.

He stared at her for a long moment, then nodded. 'Your wish is my command.'

'But I'm not usually like this,' she said shakily.

'You don't have to make excuses to me,' he replied darkly as he ushered her into the lift, then used his key card to gain access to their floor. 'I am well acquainted with the perversities of the flesh.'

Neither of them said anything during the brief ride upwards. Neither did they touch each other.

By the time the lift stopped and the doors opened, Emily felt close to fainting. When she swayed on her high heels, Sebastian scooped her up into his arms and carried her from the lift.

No one was in the waiting area to stare at them. Neither did they encounter anyone walking along the hotel corridor.

Not that Emily would have cared. Not with Sebastian's arms around her. She wrapped her own arms around his neck, her handbag hanging down his back.

When he reached their door, he moved his hold from behind her knees to just underneath her bottom, taking her full weight with that one arm whilst he used the hand which had been around her waist to open the door. Once inside, he kicked the door shut before carrying her past their bags—which had preceded them—striding through the spacious lounge room straight into the luxuriously appointed bedroom, which had a sitting area of its own and a king-sized bed covered by a cream lambswool spread.

Emily was not surprised that he'd booked what was probably one of the most expensive suites in the hotel. Men like Sebastian always travelled in style.

But she was taken aback by what she knew were not customary accoutrements, unless one asked for them. Patrons of such a suite could expect a complimentary bottle of champagne on arrival. But not a magnum, or chocolate-dipped strawberries, presented exquisitely on a delicate crystal plate.

'No,' he said brusquely when he spotted the direction of her eyes. 'None of that till later.

'I won't be long. But before I go…' Cupping the back of her head, he planted a brutal kiss on her mouth, ravaging her orally for several seconds before wrenching his mouth away. 'You could hurry things along by getting undressed,' he told her gruffly, before spinning on his heel and stalking off into the adjoining *en suite* bathroom.

Emily stared after him, her heart thudding loudly in her chest.

She supposed she was getting what she'd asked for. But, for some weird and wonderful reason, she no longer wanted rough sex.

But she could hardly complain now. He would think she was crazy, going hot and cold on him all the time.

Not that she'd gone cold. She hadn't; her body was on fire.

But she wanted Sebastian to make love to her. Her stomach flipped over. If he came out and found that she hadn't even started undressing, he might think she'd changed her mind again.

Exhaling a shaky sigh, Emily placed her handbag on the seat of a nearby chair before removing her suede jacket and draping it over the back. Despite the pleasant temperature in the room, she suddenly broke out into goose-bumps and was standing there, rubbing her upper arms with her hands, when Sebastian emerged from the bathroom.

Their eyes met, Emily's gaze pleading with him not to do what she'd asked earlier. She needed him to be gentle with her. To be tender and romantic. She needed to pretend.

No woman had ever looked at Sebastian the way Emily was looking at him at this moment.

His bed-partners of choice in recent years had invariably been beautiful and provocative creatures, confident in their bodies and their sexual know-how. He'd never been attracted to shrinking violets, or blushing virgins.

Not that Emily was either of these things. He'd discovered for himself last night, and again today, that his seemingly reserved housekeeper could be as bold as the best of them.

She was, however, extremely vulnerable at this time in her life; it shone through in her worried, wide-eyed gaze.

He supposed it could not be easy to go to bed

with a man after a break of four years. Or to strip off in front of him the way Lana would have done.

Sebastian decided that a change of tack was called for.

'There's a couple of complimentary robes in the bathroom,' he said straight away. 'Why don't you get undressed in there and put one on?'

Her relief was touchingly transparent as she swept up her handbag and hurried into the bathroom.

She was sweet, yet so damned sexy.

Sebastian hummed as he swiftly opened the magnum of champagne, poured two glasses and carried them over to the bedside table. After that, he returned to the living room, where he extracted some condoms from his overnight bag. Back in the bedroom, he put the foil packets into a bedside drawer.

Better to be safe than sorry but, with a bit of luck, by morning, Emily might be swayed into accepting his proposal and the use of protection could be dispensed with.

Of course, he'd have to impress her tonight if that was to happen.

Sebastian had no doubt he could deliver, sexually. He had every confidence in his bedroom know-how. The problem would lie with Emily's emotions. She was far more complex than he'd imagined. Far less pragmatic. And far more sensitive.

Sebastian didn't have any personal experience with soft, sensitive women.

The bathroom door opened quietly, Emily emerging wrapped from neck to ankle in a voluminous white towelling robe. Her face looked almost as white as she walked slowly back to the bed.

'Oh,' she said, her pale skin brightening once she sighted the glasses by the bed. 'You opened the champagne.'

Good move, Sebastian.

'It seemed mean not to,' he replied smoothly. 'And not very romantic. Now, why don't you slip out of that robe and pop into bed, beautiful?'

When she hesitated, he reached to undo the sash at her waist, watching her eyes whilst he parted the robe and pushed it back off her shoulders.

Sebastian thought he knew what to expect from her body. He'd seen her naked in the pool, hadn't he? He already knew she was full-breasted and much slimmer than her loose-fitting clothes had indicated.

He almost didn't glance downwards as the robe fell from her shoulders, not wanting to embarrass her at this stage.

But when her eyes dropped away from his, he automatically looked down.

Sebastian was a connoisseur of female beauty, nothing attracting him more than a woman who looked like a woman. He did not agree with the fashionable idea that a woman could never be too thin. Neither did he like females who sported pumped-up or sinewy muscles.

Emily had everything Sebastian liked and which rarely came in one package. Magnificent breasts. A tiny waist which he could put his hands around. Great child-bearing hips which balanced her bust.

And long shapely legs with slender ankles and small feet.

She possessed an hour-glass figure at its best, further complimented with a gently rounded stomach and the kind of soft clear skin which would feel great to touch.

By comparison, Lana had no mystery about her. She was a whore, Sebastian had finally come to realise. A heartless, gold-digging whore.

But not this lovely creature standing nervously before him. She couldn't be bought. That much was already obvious.

Which made Sebastian want her all the more, not just for tonight, but for the rest of his life.

So he'd better make sure he did this right.

'You are beyond beautiful, Emily,' he said softly. 'Come here…' He moved away from her to drag back the woollen spread and the crisp white bed-linen. 'Cover that far too tempting body up while I get myself undressed.'

CHAPTER TEN

A FLUSHED Emily found herself sitting up in the middle of the king-sized bed, the sheet clutched modestly over her breasts whilst she watched Sebastian undress, not in the privacy of the bathroom as she had done, but right in front of her.

His removal of his suit jacket didn't overly quicken her heartbeat, but when he yanked his black top out of the waistband of his trousers and reefed it up over his head, her pulse-rate went into overdrive. Which was ridiculous, really. She'd seen him bare-chested many times before, when he went swimming, and of course she already knew that his body was simply superb: broad shoulders, slender hips, a six-pack stomach, courtesy of all that rowing he did, and his skin was silky smooth and beautifully bronzed.

To look at him, you'd never believe he was forty.

Looking at him now, however, felt very different from looking at him around the pool, because of where it was heading—to total nudity, and him in this bed with her, touching her, kissing her, making love with her.

Emily gulped, then grabbed the champagne glass from the bedside table. A few drops spilled as she swept it up to her lips, because her eyes were not on what she was doing. They were fixed on Sebastian's hands, which had just unsnapped his waistband and unzipped the zip. Emily tried not to stare as he pushed his trousers down over his hips. But when his rough action took his underpants with him, her mouth went bone-dry.

'Better take these off too,' Sebastian said with a quick smile, then sat on the side of the bed and disposed of his shoes and socks.

'You're looking much more relaxed,' he said as he dived under the covers with her. 'Must be the champers. Give me a bit of yours.'

Both his hands closed over hers as he brought the glass to his lips. Emily stared deep into his eyes as he took a hefty swallow, an incredulous feeling rushing through her.

'This is just so crazy,' she said shakily.

Sebastian took the glass out of her hands, downed the rest of the contents, then placed it back on the bedside table. When he turned back to face her, he cupped her cheeks with his hands.

'Crazy can be good,' he said, pushing her back down on to the pillows. 'Crazy can be fun. How long is it, Emily, since you've had fun?'

'Too long,' she whispered just before his lips met hers.

Emily closed her eyes, then moaned, a low soft moan which echoed the rush of emotion which threatened to overwhelm her. Because it was finally happening. Sebastian was making love to her. Really making love to her.

His mouth was gentle. Not rough at all. And his hands. Oh, goodness, his hands...

One lifted to stroke the hair back from her forehead whilst the other travelled down her throat, over a breast, her ribs, her stomach, his touch slow and sensuous. Her skin tingled wherever he went, the rest of her body dying to have him touch her there.

But he took his time, making her wait, making her whimper each time his fingers grazed far too briefly over a stunningly erect nipple.

That roving hand finally made more intimate inroads, sliding down between her legs, bringing a tortured gasp to her lips.

Oh, no, she thought despairingly when he honed in on her most erotic zone. If he kept doing that she was going to come! And she didn't want that. She wanted him inside her. Wanted to hold him close. Wanted to be as one with him.

All her muscles stiffened, her mind desperately trying to stop the inevitable.

His withdrawing his hand brought a raw groan of relief. When his head lifted, her eyes clung to his in a mad mixture of adoration and gratitude.

He smiled down at her, then gave her a soft peck on her still parted lips.

'Won't be a sec,' he said huskily, then rolled away, yanked opened the top drawer of the bedside table and extracted a small foil packet.

His stopping to protect both of them brought

another rush of relief and gratitude. Because Emily had been way past caring if he wore a condom or not. If he'd asked her to marry him at this moment, she would have said yes like a shot.

'Now where was I?' he murmured when he rolled back.

'No, don't,' she gasped when that wickedly knowing hand swiftly re-entered the danger zone.

'You don't like that?' he questioned, his expression surprised.

'I like it too much,' she choked out.

Sebastian smiled. 'What would you like me to do, then?'

'Just do it, for pity's sake.'

His laugh was soft and wry. 'And there I was, thinking all these months that my wonderful cool and calm housekeeper was the epitome of patience. No no, don't turn your face away, Emily. I like the wild passion in your eyes. It excites me. Here, feel what you've done to me.'

His pressing her hand against his stunning erection was like opening the lid on Emily's desire. With a naked groan, she encircled him, holding him tightly whilst she caressed his rock-hard flesh.

His muttered swearword showed she'd taken him by surprise.

'Stop that,' he growled and, grabbing both her hands, drove them high against the pillows above her head. The action sent him looming over her, his naked chest rubbing against her throbbing breasts, his erection pressing into her stomach.

'Put your legs up around me,' he ordered roughly.

Once she did, he let her hands go, trusting perhaps that she would now lie still for him. But more likely because he needed his own hands elsewhere.

Emily would never forget the moment he first entered her, the rush of emotion far overwhelming any physical sensation.

Her heart lurched, but so did her body, shattering apart in an instant orgasm which was as perversely pleasurable as it was dismayingly premature. Her head whipped from side to side, her eyes squeezing tightly shut as her body trembled from top to toe.

Oh, Sebastian, she cried silently, tears welling up behind her eyelids. *My darling. My love.*

Sebastian didn't know what to do.

If he wasn't sadly mistaken, Emily was crying.

Should he ignore the fact and just continue?

His own body was screaming at him for release. At the same time, it seemed insensitive not to stop and see what was wrong. Though he suspected he already knew.

'No, no,' she choked out when he began to withdraw.

Sebastian sank back into the still throbbing depths of her body with a relieved sigh. At the same time, he did lever himself up on to his elbows so that he could see if his suspicions were correct.

Yes, she was crying, damn it. Not hysterically. Very quietly, silent tears running down her cheeks.

'You're not thinking of that fool, Mark, are you?'

he asked with a touch of exasperation. Why was it that the really sweet girls in this world always fell for selfish creeps?

'Mark?' she said blankly, her eyes blinking open. 'No. No. I...I'm not thinking of Mark.'

'What, then?'

'Can't...can't a person cry with happiness?'

'Happiness?'

'Yes. It...it's such a relief to know I can enjoy sex without love after all.'

Sebastian couldn't work out why this discovery of Emily's didn't please him as much as he thought it would. Maybe because he'd been secretly hoping she would fall in love with him, once he made love to her. It would have made his marriage mission a lot easier.

Still, it was good that she was enjoying herself and not pining after some idiot.

'Okay for me to continue then?' he asked even as he was already moving inside her.

She didn't say anything, but her mouth fell open and her eyes glazed over. She sucked in sharply when her body started gripping his, a sure sign that she was far from finished.

Sebastian was suddenly seized with the urge to show Emily that if she married him, her sex life would not be restricted to once a night, or the missionary position. He would make love to her often, and in all sorts of ways.

Starting now!

She moaned softly when he withdrew, but made no protest when he flipped her over and pulled her up on to her hands and knees. Doing it this way had always been one of Sebastian's favourite positions. Perhaps because it practically guaranteed a woman's pleasure and satisfaction.

Sebastian prided himself on his sexual expertise and control, but Emily was proving to be a strangely difficult partner for him to keep his head with.

If only she'd stop rocking back and forth on her hands and knees, stop pressing her deliciously rounded bottom hard up against his groin.

His hands reached up to cup her breasts in a vain attempt to still the rest of her body, but it was too late. He'd reached the point of no return, his head bursting with stars as his body exploded deep inside her.

He didn't expect her to come with him, but astonishingly she did, heightening the thrill of his release when her flesh started spasming around his, over and over and over.

Sebastian tried not to groan. He was not normally a noisy lover. But groan he did. And it felt wonderful.

He decided not to be so silent in future.

Carefully he withdrew, not surprised when Emily collapsed, face down, on the bed, her arms outspread, her shuddering sigh that of a sated woman.

Sebastian smiled a darkly knowing smile. If she thought the sex was over, then she was very much mistaken. It had only just begun.

He stroked a possessive hand down the lovely curve of her spine, then trailed the back of his fingers over her peach-like buttocks, pleased with the tremors that rippled through her.

Sebastian now wanted to marry Emily more than ever. He would have the best of both worlds with this woman. A peaceful life, and passion as well. What more could he want?

The thought of her accepting that job next Monday then leaving him could not be tolerated. He had to find a way to keep her with him, to make her marry him. Satisfying sex alone might not be enough to achieve that. Emily might still think she wanted love as well.

An idea popped into his head which was rather ruthless.

Could he get away with it?

Sebastian slid his hand down between her legs and played with her there till she squirmed, then moaned.

No trouble, he thought with a rush of heady power. No trouble at all.

CHAPTER ELEVEN

I MUST keep my head. I must keep my head. I must keep my head.

This mantra kept running through Emily's mind as she leant back in the spa bath, a chocolate-dipped strawberry in one hand and a fresh glass of champagne in the other.

Difficult to keep one's head, however, when one was this tipsy, and this much in love.

It was Sebastian who'd run the bath, and lit the candles, and arranged everything in here for them to eat and drink. Sebastian who'd thoughtfully given her five minutes privacy before he'd joined her in the bubble bath. Sebastian who was being so wonderfully attentive to her that if she didn't know him better, she might think he was in love with her as well!

But she understood that this was all part of his seduction routine.

'What time is it?' she asked before taking a delicious bite out of the strawberry, then following up with a sip of champagne.

'Around seven, I think,' he replied nonchalantly. 'Maybe a bit later. Are you hungry? Do you want me to order dinner from room service after we get out of here?'

'No. Not yet. I think all these strawberries have ruined my appetite.' She popped the last one into her mouth and washed it down with more champagne.

'We'll go for a walk later. Then you might feel like something more substantial than strawberries.'

Emily couldn't think of anything she'd like to do less than get dressed and go for a walk.

'Couldn't we just stay here?'

'You mean in this bath?'

'No. I'm getting a bit pruny. I was thinking that maybe…if it's all right with you…we could…um…I mean…I could…um…'

It was hard to just come out with what she wanted to do, despite being tipsy!

'Emily,' Sebastian said with that look he always got on his face when he was frustrated with something, or someone. 'Stop stammering and just say it.'

Emily took another mouthful of champagne. 'All right. I want to go back to bed and make love to *you*.'

His eyebrows lifted. 'You like being on top?'

'Well I…sometimes,' she said, even though it was a lie. She'd never overly liked that position. But she'd fantasised quite a bit lately about making love to Sebastian that way, and this might be her only chance to make that fantasy come true. It wasn't the being-on-top part she craved so much but the experience of touching him all over, and kissing him all over.

His blue eyes twinkled at her. 'Emily Bayliss, you are constantly surprising me today.'

'That's because you don't really know me. Just as I don't really know you.'

'Are you warning me again that you won't change your mind and marry me?'

Emily's hand tightened around her champagne glass. 'You promised we wouldn't talk about that tonight.'

'So I did,' he muttered. 'More fool me. But I'll be bringing the subject up again tomorrow.'

If he asked her whilst they were down here, in this romantic environment, she'd probably say yes. She could already feel her resolve to walk away weakening appreciably.

'Not till we leave here,' she asked him. 'Please, Sebastian.'

If he waited till they were on their way back to Hunter's Hill, she'd be back in reality again.

'Why's that?'

'Because I'm having a lovely time and I don't want to argue with you.'

'I can't imagine you ever arguing with anyone. Not seriously.'

'In that case, you *really* don't know me. Just before I came to work for you, I argued with my father and I haven't spoken to him since.'

Sebastian frowned. 'What on earth did you argue about?'

Emily regretted bringing her father into their conversation. Talk about an instant dampener. Although perhaps it was a timely reminder of how men used the women who loved them for their own ends. She had to be careful that she didn't let Sebastian become the third man in a row to make her into a victim.

Time to take control of your life again, Emily. Time to have what *you* want, even if it is only for tonight.

'Would you mind if I deferred any disclosures of family feuds to some other time?' she said, sliding forward to take the almost empty champagne glass out of Sebastian's hand. 'I don't think this is the time or the place. Now…'

She stood up carefully in the bath, thrilling to the look in his eyes as he glanced up at her unfolding nudity.

'I'll just get out and put these glasses down. You stay where you are till I'm nice and dry. Then I'll see to you.'

Wow, Sebastian thought as he watched Emily towel herself down, one sensual bit at a time. This is one sexy woman.

By the time he climbed out of the bath, he was fiercely erect. By the time she finished towelling him down, he wished he hadn't agreed to her taking charge of their lovemaking. The urge to hoist her up on to the vanity unit and plunge into her right here and now was so intense he had to battle for control.

Returning to the bedroom—and the bed—gave him a brief respite. But he still extracted a condom from the drawer straight away and handed it to her, hoping she'd take the hint.

She smiled a saucy little smile, then placed it on the other bedside table.

'We won't be needing that just yet,' she purred, then snuggled up to his side, her head on his right shoulder, her left hand resting in the middle of his chest.

'You're not to do a thing,' she instructed him as the hand on his chest began to move downwards in slow, tantalising circles.

Sebastian's stomach muscles tensed as she moved inexorably closer to his erection.

Her head lifted from his shoulder and she stared down at him for a long moment whilst her fingertips traced the muscles between his ribs. Her eyes were glazed, her expression almost wistful.

'You have a magnificent body, Sebastian,' she said at last.

'I work hard at it,' he replied, whilst thinking that Lana had never once given him a compliment like that. She'd been the one who expected all the compliments.

'What are you going to do in the morning with no river to row on?' Emily murmured.

'The same thing I do when I'm away.'

She glanced up at him, her hand stilling once more. 'Which is what?'

'A hundred push-ups and a five kilometre run.'

'You're kidding me.'

'No.'

'That's a bit obsessive, don't you think?'

'I *am* obsessive. How else would I have been the success I've been?'

'Maybe it's time for you to relax a little and enjoy the fruits of your labour.'

'Difficult to relax right at this precise moment,' he said with a stifled groan when the side of her hand brushed the tip of his erection.

'Poor darling,' Emily said throatily.

Sebastian knew where she was heading when she sat up and wriggled around to lie sidewards on the bed, both her head and hands having easy access to his lower body. Clearly, she meant to go down on him. Maybe even go all the way.

Strangely, Sebastian wasn't that fond of fellatio. He'd never been really convinced that a woman enjoyed doing it. Since becoming rich, he'd had any number of women all too eager to go down on him.

And, whilst he could not deny it gave him physical pleasure, he always felt mentally distanced from the act, his one overriding emotion being cynicism.

But as Emily caressed him intimately, then put her lips where her hands had been, Sebastian's heart squeezed tight. Impossible to feel cynical about this woman's lovemaking. Emily had no materialistic motive in giving him oral sex. There was no artifice in her, or cold-blooded ambition. She was doing this for pure pleasure. His and hers.

He moaned under the impact of the soft kisses she rained up and down his shaft, stunned by the feelings she evoked in him. When she finally sucked him deep into her mouth, he was propelled into a maelstrom of sensation and emotion which was totally alien to him.

He could hardly think. Hardly breathe.

Coming was only a heartbeat away when she stopped, pushing her hair out of her face as she looked up at him with a heavy-lidded gaze.

'I won't stop if you don't want me to,' she said.

Sebastian stared at her wet lips. At her flushed face. At her fiercely erect nipples.

'It's up to you,' he replied thickly.

'I'd rather do this,' she whispered, and moved to straddle him, her hands shaking as she angled his aching flesh into her body.

He groaned at the heat of her. And the wetness. She sank down upon him to the hilt, then began to rise and fall in a most abandoned rhythm.

Sebastian could see that she'd forgotten all about protection. She was lost to her passion and her need. Lost to the heat of the moment.

He wasn't far behind.

He momentarily thought of his earlier ruthless resolve to have unsafe sex with her before the night was out, to do his best to make her pregnant, thereby ensuring that she would marry him.

All of a sudden, however, it didn't seem right to try to trap her. Or to let her trap herself. Emily deserved better than that. So did any child they might or might not have in the future.

Sebastian frowned, his mind swinging abruptly to the serious subject of procreation.

He'd shied away from having children in the past, mostly because he'd needed all his focus and energy to make a success of his life. But partly because he'd never had a relationship with a woman he'd felt confident of being a really good mother.

Whilst he knew Emily was just such a woman, he still wanted her to be his wife before she conceived. He never wanted any child of his to have any reason to criticise his parents. Or to feel the kind of negative emotions he'd felt whilst growing up. A child deserved to be wanted and loved right from the beginning, not used as an instrument of emotional blackmail.

Which left Sebastian no option but to revert to his original plan, that of binding Emily to him sexually this weekend so that she could not possibly say no when he asked her again to marry him. It was obvious she was enjoying being on top, but that was not the kind of sex which would achieve his aim. He needed to take command again, needed to give her a level of pleasure which she'd hopefully never experienced with any other man.

When he took her forcibly by her hips and lifted her right off him, she cried out. Whether in surprise or protest, he wasn't sure. But it really didn't matter.

'Time for a change, beautiful,' he growled as he tossed her on to the bed, then loomed over her, bending his head to one of her fiercely erect nipples, licking it, then tugging at it with his teeth. She sucked in sharply, then moaned with pleasure, reminding him of what she'd said to him earlier in the afternoon.

'Don't be gentle with me...'

He aimed to take her at her word this time, moving over to her other breast, where he gave her eagerly awaiting nipple the same rough treatment. Only when her breasts had to be burning did he abandon them, sliding slowly down her body, sucking and biting her stomach as he went.

Even before his mouth reached its destination, her legs had fallen wantonly apart, evidence of her fever-pitch arousal. When he stabbed his tongue against her swollen clitoris, she immediately splintered apart, crying out her release.

'No, no,' she whimpered when he kept going, a sure indication that no man had done this to her before, taken her beyond that moment when she thought she wanted him to stop, propelling her to a blissfully erotic place where her mind was no longer connected to her body, where her flesh reacted instinctively, like an animal in heat.

She came and she came, moaning softly each time, till at last she lay still, totally spent. Or so she thought.

Sebastian immediately knelt up between her thighs, leaning over to snatch up the condom from the bedside table. She cried out when he pulled her up from the bed and slid her roughly across his thighs. Cried out again when he drove into her.

Her big blue eyes met his, their expression dazed.

'No more,' she said brokenly. 'No more…' And her head flopped forward against his chest, her arms dangling limply by her sides.

He ignored her, cupping her buttocks with his hands and rocking her back and forth upon him, clenching his teeth hard in his jaw in an effort to harness his rapidly disintegrating control.

A sigh whispered from her lips, but she did not

protest, her body deliciously soft and compliant. He knew he could not possibly last long. Yet somehow he managed to hold on whilst his mind willed her to respond. Because he knew if she did...if she could not resist...if her body could be made to crave yet another orgasm, then she would be his.

Her arms were the first part of her to come to life, lifting from her sides to wrap around his back. Then it was her lips nuzzling at his neck. Then her internal muscles, clasping and releasing him in that way women's bodies did when they were well on their way to orgasm.

Finally, she began digging her knees into the bed and grinding herself against him. Her head jerked up and tipped back, her spine arching, her mouth gasping wide open as she took him with her in a release which had him bellowing like a bull.

Sebastian had never experienced anything like it.

Clutching her tightly against his chest, he buried his face in her hair, his flesh finally free to lose itself in hers. Which it did, for what felt like an interminable time, his spasms not stopping till long after hers.

Her having fallen asleep in his arms went unnoticed till he called her name and received no answer.

Sebastian smiled a triumphant smile, then lowered her gently back to the bed, satisfied that his mission had just about been completed.

Not that he intended to rest on his laurels.

Emily was not the sort of girl whose mind could be easily swayed or changed. He would have to re-inforce his sexual hold over her when she woke, his ultimate mission being to make her totally addicted to his lovemaking before this night was out.

Not an unpleasant prospect, he conceded as he withdrew. Emily was proving herself to be a very intriguing bed partner. Marriage to her would certainly be more than a marriage of convenience. It would be both relaxing and exciting at the same time.

She sighed in her sleep when he stroked a soft hand over her breasts, her belly, her bottom. Sighed, then quivered.

A new wave of triumph washed through Sebastian as he realised she was responding to him, even when her mind was completely shut down. He might have played with her further if he hadn't been exhausted himself. Frankly, he needed a rest if he was going to keep proving himself the exceptional lover he'd bragged about being.

But Sebastian found it difficult to take his hands from her body, difficult to leave her.

Emily *had* to marry him, he decided fiercely when he finally forced himself to rise and head for the bathroom.

Come tomorrow, he would not take no for an answer!

CHAPTER TWELVE

'ANOTHER cup of coffee?' Sebastian asked Emily as he picked up the stainless steel pot and poured himself some more.

They were sitting out on the sun-drenched balcony, wrapped in matching robes, having just finished the very substantial breakfast Sebastian had ordered the night before and which had been delivered to their suite on a beautifully appointed trolley.

'Yes, please,' Emily replied, thinking to herself that Sebastian was still pulling out all stops to impress her. She'd never seen him once offer to pour Lana more coffee.

There again, he'd never wanted to marry Lana.

But does he still want to marry me? came the sudden thought.

Sebastian hadn't brought the matter up again this morning. And he would have if he wanted to, regardless of her asking him to leave any discussion of marriage till they left here. Maybe, after last night's performance, he didn't think he had to offer marriage to stop her from leaving. Maybe he believed she'd settle for being his mistress instead.

Which she probably would, Emily conceded unhappily.

'That's enough, thank you,' she said when her coffee cup was three-quarters full. Ironic words, ones which she wished she'd been capable of saying a couple of times last night.

Emily had known she was taking a risk agreeing to spend the night with the man she loved. She hadn't realised, however, how great a risk it was. By the time she'd woken this morning, any resolve she'd had to just walk away had well and truly dissolved, replaced by an all-consuming need to just be with him, no matter what.

Emily shivered at the memory of everything she'd experienced in his arms. She'd thought Mark had been good in bed. By comparison, Mark had been a novice, with limited imagination and stamina. Sebastian had shown her that a night spent with him went way beyond the romantic fantasy she'd envisaged.

Emily had never known such a dominating and demanding lover. He had not just made love to her countless times in countless ways. He'd skilfully seduced her mind along with her body till she wanted him continuously, unable to say no to anything he suggested.

Even now, sitting here, sipping coffee, she wanted him. Yet less than half an hour ago they'd been making love, on the vanity unit top, her body still dripping wet from the erotically charged shower they'd just shared.

She should have been satisfied. Instead, she wanted more.

Sebastian had uncovered a level of sensuality in her which she'd never known she possessed. And now…now she was totally at his mercy.

Her only defence was pretence. So she was doing her best to act like a sophisticated woman of the world who'd been there, done that.

Who knew? Maybe she would still find the courage to walk away.

But she seriously doubted it.

The room telephone suddenly ringing brought a scowl to Sebastian's face. He put down the coffee pot and stood up, retying his towelling robe as he did so.

'I hope that's not reception forgetting we have late checkout,' he muttered as he headed inside.

Emily stood up also, but not to go inside. She walked over to the balcony railing, taking her coffee with her, sipping it slowly as she tried to find distraction from her worrying thoughts by surveying the picturesque view.

It looked spectacular in the morning light, the ocean sparkling under the rising sun. From the height of their floor, she could see above the tops of the Norfolk pines which lined the beach below, right out to the distant horizon.

It was inevitable, however, that her gaze was drawn down to the path which followed the pines and along which they'd walked the previous evening. They'd not long shared a lovely meal—brought by room service, of course—when Sebastian had suggested a stroll along the harbourside paths. She'd jumped at the chance, because by then she'd started to be consumed by the disturbing need to have him inside her all the time. She'd hoped that time away from that seductive hotel suite might break the cycle of need.

Wishful thinking…

Emily stared down at the path, wondering which pine tree it was that he'd pulled her over to, leaning her back up against the trunk whilst he'd kissed and fondled her. They must have looked like necking teenagers, or possibly honeymooners, unable to keep their hands off each other. The shadow of the tree had provided some privacy from passers-by. But people could probably have still seen them.

Yet Emily hadn't cared. She'd thrilled to his hands on her breasts, her bottom. Only when he'd reduced her to begging him for more intimacy, did he lead her back to the hotel for more.

'Damn and blast!' Sebastian muttered as he strode back on to the balcony, looking irritated and exasperated.

'What's wrong?'

'That wasn't reception. It was John.'

'John? Oh, you mean your PA.'

'I told him where I was heading in case I didn't come back. I always tell someone my destination when I drive off somewhere. I usually tell you, but you were coming with me. Not that I told him that.'

Emily wondered why not, if he was serious about marrying her.

'He couldn't contact me on my mobile, since I turned it off, so he had to ring here.'

'A business emergency, I presume?' she ventured.

Sebastian was a hands-on company owner who didn't delegate well. He was always being rung at home by various company executives, who all seemed to work seven days a week.

'There's a problem with a retirement village I'm building in Queensland,' he explained, frustration in his voice and in his face.

'What kind of problem?'

'What? Oh, nothing to worry your pretty little head about.' His frown cleared, his mouth curving into a sexy smile as he walked over to her. 'Mmm... You do look delicious in this robe,' he said, moving around behind her and wrapping his arms around her waist. 'But you look better without it.'

Emily could not believe it when he started undoing the sash. 'Sebastian! Stop that!' she protested, panic-stricken at the way her heart immediately started to race. 'Now look what you've done. You've made me spill my coffee.'

'Drink it up, then.'

'How can I possibly drink coffee with you undressing me? Sebastian! Someone might see!'

'Would you like that?' he purred into her ear as he opened the robe wide then cupped his hands over her breasts. 'Does that turn you on, Emily? The thought of having someone watch me make love to you? It turned you on last night, down there, against that tree.'

'You're a wicked man,' she choked out, clasping the mug more tightly between both hands.

'You're the wicked one,' he growled. 'You, and this provocative body of yours. It does things to me, Emily. *You* do things to me. I can't get enough of you.'

'You shouldn't say such things.'

Or *do* such things, she thought breathlessly. He'd retied the robe, but lifted the hem at the back and tucked it into the sash at her waist.

'Why not?' he said thickly, his hands stroking over her bare buttocks. 'They're true.'

Emily stiffened when his hands dropped down to the back of her thighs, then came up between them.

'Sebastian, no,' she pleaded, even as her whole body trembled. 'Please stop.'

The anguished note in her voice finally got through to Sebastian. Not an easy thing to do at that precise moment. He really meant it when he said he couldn't get enough of her.

He couldn't.

His success with her last night had really gone to his head. Even this morning, he'd needed the fix of her surrendering to him one more time. And now, here he was, needing it again, despite having surely proved their sexual compatibility by now.

If he ignored her protest and succeeded in seducing her against her will, things might backfire on him. As much as he wanted Emily again—with an addictive passion which superseded anything he'd felt with Lana—he wanted her as his wife even more.

'Fine,' he said through gritted teeth, and yanked the robe back down. 'I would never do anything you didn't want, Emily. But it might be wise if we removed temptation by getting dressed, then getting the hell out of here.'

He hadn't meant to speak in such a harsh tone, but damn it all, he was more frustrated than he could ever remember.

She whirled around, her face flushed, her big blue eyes dilated with desire.

'It's not that I don't want you to make love to me. I do,' she confessed shakily. 'Just…just not out here. And not like that.'

Aaah. So it was romance she was after now. Sebastian took the coffee cup out of her hands and put it on the balcony railing. He could do romance. When he had to.

But first…

Her eyes widened when he undid the robe again, then stripped it from her body. Sebastian feasted his eyes on her voluptuous curves before sweeping her up into his arms and carrying her inside.

One hour later, Emily was sitting silently in the passenger seat of Sebastian's car as they left the hotel, certain that any offer of marriage was now not on Sebastian's agenda. He'd had every opportunity to mention it. But he'd gone quiet after their last love-making, a ridiculously tender episode which had left Emily close to tears. She would have rather him ravage her than make love to her in such a gentle fashion, his eyes never leaving hers from the moment he entered her.

What had he been hoping to see?

Whatever, she'd denied him the satisfaction of witnessing her umpteenth capitulation by closing her eyes and coming very quietly. Afterwards, she'd dressed without saying a word, then accompanied him downstairs in a state of almost weary resignation to her fate.

Loving Mark had brought her heartache and bitterness. Loving her father had brought her dismay and disappointment. Loving Sebastian was going to bring her to a depth of despair she could hardly imagine.

Because he would never ever love her back.

'I'm taking the coast road back,' Sebastian explained when he turned down a different road from the way they'd come. 'I want to show you the new Sea Cliff bridge. It's quite spectacular,' he added with a smile, his first for ages. 'You haven't seen it already, have you?'

'Only on the television,' Emily replied, her low spirits immediately lifting.

Even on the TV it had looked truly amazing, a huge serpentine construction which followed the cliffs, but away from the fragile escarpment where rock falls were common. At one point it even snaked out over the ocean itself.

'We'll stop and walk across it,' Sebastian went on. 'There's a pedestrian path for sightseeing.'

'I'd love that,' Emily said sincerely, taken aback but pleased by his suggestion. 'Just as well I wore my jeans and joggers.'

It didn't take very long to reach the bridge, and it was truly amazing. All too quickly, however, they'd driven over it, Emily appreciating that Sebastian wouldn't have seen much at all, having to keep his eyes on the road.

At the northern end of the bridge there was a parking area to one side for people who wanted to walk the bridge. Sebastian turned into it and parked next to a small bus, out of which a group of Japanese tourists were pouring.

'What a pity we don't have a camera,' Emily said when she saw all the Japanese tourists taking snaps of everything.

'Wait here,' Sebastian said and walked over to a Japanese man who had three cameras hanging round his neck. After a brief conversation and an exchange of money, he came back with a camera.

'Fire away,' he said as he handed it to her. 'It's digital and simple. You just look through there and if you like the shot, press that button.'

'You speak Japanese?' she asked, amazed.

'I had to go to Tokyo on business a couple of years back and thought it best to learn. Damned hard language to master.'

But he would have mastered it, Emily realised ruefully, just as he mastered everything he set his mind to. He'd mastered her last night all right.

'Come on,' he said after she'd snapped a few shots. 'Put that around your neck and let's walk.'

They made it across from one side to the other in about fifteen minutes, though they didn't rush. On the way back, Sebastian stopped at a point where, when you looked over the side, far below you could see the sea crashing on to rocks. Emily took some photos of the spray hitting the base of the concrete pier, then of the ships on the horizon. There were lots of them, huge tankers and cargo vessels. The larger south coast towns were sea ports, which shipped out coal and steel.

'All finished?' Sebastian asked when she finally took the camera away from her eyes.

'Yes. I'll put them up on my computer tonight and...oh!' she gasped.

There, sitting on the railing in front of Sebastian, was an open ring box containing what had to be the biggest diamond ring she'd ever seen.

CHAPTER THIRTEEN

'MY GOD!' Emily said, turning stunned eyes to him. 'Where…where did that come from?'

'I bought it yesterday morning when I went into the city.'

Emily blinked. He'd bought it *yesterday*?

'I would have given it to you over breakfast, but you made me promise not to mention marriage again till we left the hotel. Well, we've left the hotel, Emily,' he said, picking up the box and holding it out to her. 'So I'm asking you again. Will you marry me?'

Shock held Emily speechless for a long moment. She'd been so sure he wasn't going to ask her.

'You…you really are too much, Sebastian,' she heard herself babbling. 'To buy a ring like that before you even proposed.'

'I presumed you'd say yes.'

'It must have cost you a fortune!'

'A quarter of a million.'

Emily's mouth dropped open.

'It's no more than you deserve,' he said. 'You're

a very special woman, Emily. Very special indeed. I want you to be my wife more than anything I have wanted in a long time.'

Emily stared at him. Did he really mean that?

She would be foolish to believe everything he said to her. Or to misinterpret what he said. What Sebastian wanted more than anything was for his life to go along as smoothly as before, when she was taking care of his house and Lana was sharing his bed. The only difference now was that she would be doing both jobs. And yes, she would have a new title. That of wife, rather than housekeeper.

'And if I still say no?' she blurted out.

His head jerked back in surprise, his eyes darkening. 'Then this ring will be consigned to the depths of the Pacific Ocean.'

'What? Are you insane?'

'Not at all,' he bit out. 'What would you expect me to do? Return it to the jewellery shop and ask for my money back? Or keep it on the off chance I might propose to another woman in the future? I don't think so, Emily. I don't think so at all. So what is it to be? Your finger or Davy Jones's locker?'

Emily groaned. 'You really are a wicked man. You know I can't let you throw it away.'

'Then you're saying yes?'

'Yes,' she said with a shudder of defeat.

Was she mistaken or did he sigh with relief as he took the ring out of the box and slipped it on her finger?

His tossing the box away startled her, as did his

raising her left hand to his lips. A strangely old-fashioned gesture, she thought. But rather sweet.

Afterwards, he put his arm around her shoulders and started leading her back across the rest of the bridge, talking to her as they walked.

'You won't regret your decision, Emily. What we shared last night was incredible. It proved that we are sexually compatible, which was one of your main objections. As for my being ruthless...I am a tough businessman, but I never act unethically. I am also very loyal by nature. I promise I will be faithful to you. I will stand by you no matter what. I will care about you and commit myself only to you. You have my solemn word.'

Emily was touched by his speech, but glad that he didn't mention love, because she simply would not have believed him.

Who knew? Maybe their marriage did have a chance of happiness.

Whatever, she was committed to the union now and, once committed, Emily aimed to do her best to make it work. She was not a person to be half-hearted about anything she did.

They were nearing Sebastian's car when his cellphone rang. Emily knew it was his, because she recognised the tune.

'I thought you'd turned that off,' she said when he stopped to fish the phone out of his trouser pocket.

'I turned it back on before I left the hotel. Here, take my car key and get in while I answer this call.'

Emily heard him say, 'Yes, John,' before he could

possibly have known who it was on the other end. So he'd been expecting this call.

Emily sat in the car, fiddling with her ring and watching Sebastian through the windscreen. The exasperated look on his face was a bit worrying. Clearly, things in Queensland were not going well. After a few minutes, he put the phone away and strode back to the car, his expression frustrated.

'I have to go away,' he said as he climbed in behind the wheel.

'Oh, no. When?'

'This afternoon. John's booking me a flight to Brisbane, then a car to take me to Noosa.'

'Noosa,' she repeated with a sigh. That was even further away. 'When will you be back?'

'Not sure at this stage,' Sebastian said as he gunned the engine and backed out of their parking spot. 'Depends how long it will take to fix the problem. With a bit of luck I might be back tomorrow evening.'

'Oh…' Impossible to keep the disappointment out of her voice.

He slanted her a sharp look before driving off. 'Don't go imagining that I want to go, Emily. I don't. I'd much prefer to stay home with you.'

Then don't go, her heart screamed at him. Let someone else do it. Send John.

For a good minute neither of them said anything further.

It was Sebastian who spoke first. 'Look,' he said. 'I'm a businessman. And a highly successful one. I didn't get that way by being lazy or sloppy. Or letting my lesser lights do my job for me. Besides, I'm the only one who has the immediate clout to fix this problem.'

'And what problem is that, exactly?' she countered, doing her best to replicate his matter-of-fact tone and not get all emotional on him. She knew he would hate that. 'I realise that when I was your housekeeper you didn't have to explain yourself to me. But I think, as your fiancée, I have the right to be confided in a little more.'

She could see that he was taken aback by her stance. But eventually his head nodded.

'You're right,' he said. 'I'm not used to answering to anyone. I've come and gone as I pleased for years. But I can see that has to change. What would you like to know?'

'Just what the problem is. And how you're going to fix it.'

'Right. Well, I'm building these luxury retirement homes in Noosa and we got behind schedule because of some bad weather. Unfortunately, a lot of people bought these villas off the plan and their contract says they can move in next month. I organised for the builders to work seven days a week to catch up, but the foreman has suddenly walked off the job, wanting a bigger bonus. Now the rest of the men have walked, making similar demands. It's a case of blatant blackmail. I should just tell them all to get lost and hire another construction team, but that takes time and won't get these retirees into their villas on time. Lots of businessmen might not care about that, but I do. My word is my bond and I gave my word.'

Emily felt very proud of him at that moment, and slightly more confident that their marriage might just work.

'Then you must go,' she urged. 'But please... hurry back.'

'I fully intend to,' he said, and shot her the sexiest smile.

Her stomach flipped over. 'Will...will you have to leave as soon as we get home?'

'Pretty well.'

'Oh...'

'Does that "oh" mean what I think it means?'

'What do you think it means?'

He smiled. 'Don't worry. I'll do my best to make good time and give us a few minutes alone together.'

'Just a few minutes?'

'Ravishment doesn't take long.'

Heat zoomed into Emily's cheeks.

Sebastian shook his head at her. 'You like it quick sometimes, so don't pretend you don't. That's one thing I never want you to do, Emily. Be less than honest with me. I like the calm, capable woman who runs my house. But I also like the wildly passionate woman you become in my arms. There will be no room for embarrassment or inhibitions in our sex life. Do I make myself clear?'

'Yes,' she said, secretly thrilled by his words.

'Now, is there anything *you'd* like to say to me about our future sex life? Anything you like or don't like?'

Lord, there wasn't anything she didn't like with

him. There was one thing, however, which was going to bother her. Big time.

'Would it be all right if I bought a new bed for your room tomorrow? The one you have reeks of Lana's perfume.'

'New bed. New carpet. New everything, if you like. Be my guest.'

'But I can't get all that done in one day!' she protested.

'I suppose not. No worries. We'll bunk down in one of the guest rooms till it's all done.'

'One of the guest rooms,' she repeated, startled.

'You don't expect me to share that dinky little four-poster bed of yours, do you?'

'No…'

'Not that I intend to confine our sex life to beds and bedrooms.'

Emily's head whirled as her bottom squirmed. She really had to get their conversation—and her thoughts—off sex.

'I think I'll go to the hairdressers' tomorrow,' she said abruptly. 'Have my hair cut and lightened.'

He glanced over at her. 'You mean I'll be coming back to a glamorous blonde?'

'I don't know about glamorous…'

'You could be seriously glamorous, if you want to be. You have all the right equipment.'

'I will have to glam myself up before I marry you, Sebastian.'

'I actually like you as you are, Emily. But I know women. Their self esteem seems irrevocably tied in with how they look. When I get back, I'll organise a credit card for you and you can go to town on your wardrobe as well.'

Emily frowned. 'I do have some money of my own, Sebastian. I've hardly spent a cent on myself since I started working for you.'

'I have to confess, I do like it that you're not marrying me for my money. But let's be honest. As my fiancée, and then my wife, you'll be going lots of places with me. The other women there will think me a miser if my wife isn't decked out in the latest designer fashion. So humour me, will you, and let me pay for your clothes, and whatever else you might need.'

Emily sighed. 'I don't think I've thought out what marrying you will fully entail, Sebastian. It sounds complicated, being the wife of a magnate.'

'You'll manage.'

Would she?

Suddenly, Emily wished her mother was alive. She really needed to talk to someone—someone who cared about her and wouldn't just give lip service to her concerns.

It was appalling to think that she had no one to confide in. No girl-friend. No relative. She wasn't close to any of her aunts and uncles, perhaps because none of them lived in Sydney. All her grandparents had passed away, her parents not having been all that young when they'd married and had her, their only child.

Before she'd found out the awful truth, she might have asked her father what he thought of her marrying a rich man who didn't love her. There'd been a time when she'd believed him to be a wonderful man. A warm, caring, compassionate person who'd chosen to become a doctor because he had a vocation to help people.

Her mother had believed the same thing. It was a relief to Emily that her mother had never had her eyes opened to the truth about the man she'd married.

'You've gone all quiet on me,' Sebastian said. 'Are you tired?'

'Positively wrecked,' Emily replied. 'You must be too.'

'I was, till you agreed to marry me. Now I feel I could conquer the world. And hopefully make that idiot foreman get back to work,' he added wryly.

'What will you do? Read him the riot act?'

'I can't afford to get into any protracted arguments or negotiations. I'll just make him an offer he can't refuse.'

Emily stared down at her ring and wondered if that was what that had been. The offer she could not refuse.

'I'll make sure I'm home by tomorrow evening,' Sebastian said. 'And I'll take you out somewhere to celebrate our engagement.'

'Don't be silly. You'll be way too tired. I'll cook us something nice at home.'

Sebastian shook his head. 'I appreciate your consideration, but no. We'll go out. So get yourself a good night's sleep, then hit the shops tomorrow and buy yourself something seriously sexy.'

Emily's blood fizzed with a whoosh of excited anticipation. She was sitting there, making mental plans for the next day, when Sebastian leant over and gently touched her arm.

'Yes?' she said, her head whipping round in his direction.

He smiled softly at her before returning his eyes to the road.

'Now that we're engaged, would you mind telling me what you argued with your father about? You don't have to, but I'm curious. You don't seem the family feuding type.'

Emily sighed. 'Actually, I was just thinking about him a couple of minutes ago.'

'When you went all quiet on me?'

'Yes.'

'What did he do, Emily?'

'He started an affair with a colleague. *Before* Mum died. Dr Barbra Saxby. Blonde and beautiful and young enough to be his daughter. Of course, I wasn't supposed to ever find out. But I'd stayed on at home after the funeral. I wasn't in a fit state to join the workforce. I felt too depressed. Dad pretended he was doing me a favour, but I saw later that it suited him, having me there to cook and clean for him. Anyway, when I was out shopping one day, I saw them having lunch together in a restaurant. You didn't have to look too hard to see that it wasn't a business lunch.'

Emily still couldn't think of that moment without reliving the shock—and the distress—she'd felt on seeing that woman all over her father like a rash. It had only been a few weeks after her mother had passed away, after all.

'What did you do?' Sebastian asked.

'That night I confronted Dad with what I'd seen. Initially, he claimed there'd been nothing between them before Mum died, but I knew he was lying. Eventually, I wheedled the truth out of him. He broke down and said that he'd needed the comfort of a woman. He claimed he still loved Mum and would always love her. But life went on and he couldn't spend the rest of his alone. He said he was going to marry Barbra and that was that.'

'I see,' Sebastian said. 'I can imagine you were very upset.'

'That's putting it mildly. All the neighbourhood must have heard me screaming at him. I totally lost it, I can tell you. That night, I packed my bags and moved out. I stayed at a cheap motel and started looking for work. I still didn't feel like getting back into the hospitality industry. I couldn't face having to be bright and breezy with everyone. When the employment agency suggested the position as your housekeeper, I jumped at it.'

Sebastian nodded. 'Now I know why you seemed so sad at times when you first came to work for me. And why you have trust issues with men. First your boyfriend, and then your father. You know, I tried to find out some more about your background when you had a drink with me occasionally, but you always steered the conversation away from anything personal.'

'Did I? I didn't do it on purpose. It must have been subconscious.'

'No one likes to talk about the skeletons in one's closet.'

'You sound like you have a few.'

'Who, me? No, no. I was just talking in general.'

Emily didn't believe him. There was something he was hiding from her. Something in his past which had hurt him.

'So what about *your* parents?' she asked, feeling she had the right to know something of his up-bringing.

'What about them?'

'Are they still alive? They never visit, if they are.'

'They were killed in a car accident when I was eleven.'

'Oh, Sebastian, that's dreadful! You must have been traumatised.'

'It wasn't a pleasant experience. But I got over it.'

Emily stared over at him. How typically male to dismiss such a tragedy with a few understated words.

'My grandmother took me in,' he went on before she asked. 'She was a wonderful woman. You remind me of her, you know?'

'Your *grandmother*? Well, thank you very much!'

He laughed. 'Not in looks. In your calm demea-nour.'

'You keep saying how calm I am. I'm not always so calm. I learned a degree of composure when I worked on reception at the Regency. You come across some difficult clients in the hospitality industry, I can tell you. And of course I had to keep a tight rein on my emotions when I was nursing my mother. It wouldn't have helped her if I'd gone around crying all the time. Which was what I wanted to do.'

'It's not such a bad thing. To learn to control one's emotions.'

'I suppose not. I presume your grandmother has passed away?'

'Unfortunately, yes. Just before I made my first million. I would have loved to have bought her the world. Not that she probably would have appreciated it,' Sebastian added with a warm smile in his voice. 'Gran didn't hanker for material things.'

'They're not the be-all and end-all,' Emily said.

'Maybe not. But when you've been as poor as I've been, Emily, you feel differently about money. People like me go one of two ways. You either fall by the wayside or you're driven to succeed.'

'Well, you certainly succeeded. But there comes a time, Sebastian, when enough is enough. Maybe you should slow down a bit.'

'I intend to. With you. And our children.'

'Our *children*? You mean you want more than one?'

'Absolutely. If I'm going to take the plunge into fatherhood, I wouldn't want to have just one. It's too lonely for the child. Which reminds me. Now that we're getting married, do you think we could dispense with the condoms? Or am I going too quick for you again?'

Emily shook her head at him in disbelief. 'Are you always this decisive?'

'Pretty much so. But maybe I should mention that I've run out of condoms and we don't have the time to stop and buy some more.'

'That's blackmail!'

'No,' he said with a sexy grin. 'That's negotiation. So is it full steam ahead with the baby-making project before I have to jet off into the wide blue yonder?'

'You always make it impossible for me to say no!'

'Come now. You want to say yes. You know you do.'

She closed her eyes, then sighed. 'Very well. Yes…'

CHAPTER FOURTEEN

'Wow!' the hairdresser exclaimed when his job was finished. 'Here. Let me show you the back.' And he held up the mirror so that Emily could see the back of her new hair-do.

'Oh, yes,' she replied happily. 'You've done a wonderful job, Ty. Thank you so much.'

'You know, sweetie, I wasn't too sure when you came in this morning and asked me to cut your hair short, then colour it blonde. But you were right. It looks fabulous on you.'

It did. It really did. And she did have an elegant neck. Truly, she looked ten years younger, and very much in fashion.

Which reminded her of her less than fashionable wardrobe, not to mention Sebastian's request that she buy something seriously sexy for tonight.

'I'm going to hit the shops now,' she said happily as she picked up her handbag and stood up. 'I need some new clothes to go with my new look.'

'And your newly engaged status,' Ty said with a

pointed glance at her ring as they walked over to the desk together.

'Oh. You noticed,' Emily said, genuinely surprised. She'd only been to this hairdresser twice before. Once for a trim a few months back, then last week when she'd been going for that interview.

Of course, hairdressers were observant people. Especially gay ones, which Ty obviously was.

'Hard not to notice a rock like that, sweetie. Looks like you've landed yourself a real prize.'

'He's my boss.'

'The one you were planning on leaving?'

Emily realised she must have chattered away quite a bit at the hairdresser's last week. She did that when she was nervous.

'Yes, that one,' she admitted.

Ty's finely plucked eyebrows arched. 'The mobile phone magnate?'

Emily winced. What *hadn't* she told him?

She nodded as she handed over her credit card.

'Ooh,' Ty said with tightly pursed lips. 'Clever girl.'

'I'm not marrying him for his money, Ty.'

The hairdresser's dark eyes gleamed knowingly. 'Of course not. Now, when I do your hair for your wedding don't forget to mention this salon's name to all and sundry.'

Emily laughed. 'You're a wicked opportunist.'

'Takes one to know one, sweetie. Now, sign here.' And he placed the credit slip on top of the counter.

A wicked opportunist?

Emily thought about that description of herself as she walked from the salon. Was that how the cleaner had viewed her this morning when Emily had revealed she'd become engaged to Sebastian over the weekend?

Julie hadn't said much, but she'd had a look in her eyes not dissimilar to Ty's.

Emily supposed there might be quite a lot of people who thought the same thing. She wouldn't be the first housekeeper to snare her wealthy employer as a husband, the same way some female secretaries did, both having the opportunity to use their close-quarter jobs as a stepping stone to further intimacy.

But anyone who knows me would not think that, she reasoned.

But who of Sebastian's friends and employees really knows me?

None of them.

All they know is my housekeeper image, the one with the mousy hair and clothes and person-ality to match.

If I suddenly show up on Sebastian's arm, all glammed up, they're sure to think I'm a gold-digger. At the same time, I can't marry Sebastian looking frumpy.

I'm damned if I do, and damned if I don't.

Her cellphone suddenly ringing had Emily's heart leaping and her hands diving into her bag. It had to be Sebastian, letting her know when he'd be coming home. He'd rung her last night once he'd got off the plane, then again this morning, insisting that when she went out today she take her mobile with her.

'Yes?' she said, heart fluttering.

'Where are you?'

It *was* Sebastian.

'Down at Birkenhead Point.'

'Shopping for a new dress?'

'For a whole new wardrobe.'

'In one day? I doubt you'll manage that.'

'You could be right. I've just spent all morning having my hair done.'

'How does it look?'

'I think you'll like it.'

'Did you ring that employment agency and tell them you weren't accepting that job?'

'Yes. They weren't too pleased.'

'They'll get over it.'

'How are things going up there?' she asked.

'I've already persuaded the foreman back on the job, for a price. But I don't want to leave prematurely. I'm going to talk to all the other workers this afternoon and offer them bonuses as well, if they bring this job in on time. I don't want to be running back up here next week, when things go pear-shaped again. Which they might if that idiot foreman opens his big mouth and blabs about his extra bonus.'

Emily's heart sank. 'Does that mean you won't be home tonight?'

'Are you kidding? Wild horses won't keep me away. I just can't guarantee my time of arrival. At the moment I'm booked on a plane which will get me home around eight. But there's one an hour earlier. If I can make that one, I will. But it's doubtful.'

'That's all right, as long as you make it tonight. Do you want me to book somewhere for dinner?'

'Nope. That's my job, one I can easily do from here. Now, go get yourself that new dress, and if you spot a bed you like, buy that as well. I'll pay you back, of course.'

'I'd rather you be with me when I go bed-buying. You did say I could change everything in that room, remember? I wouldn't want to choose anything you didn't like.'

'Fair enough. I'd better get going.'

'Sebastian…'

'Yes?'

I love you teetered on the tip of her tongue.

'I miss you,' she said instead.

'I miss you too. That's why I'm bending over backwards to settle this today.'

'Ring me if things go wrong and you can't make it.'

'That won't happen. Have a good day now, and don't stint on what you buy.'

She didn't stint. She was downright extravagant, having to make two trips back to the car park with all her parcels. She bought more clothes and accessories in that afternoon than she had in the last five years. Fortunately, she had a healthy limit on her credit card. But she spent right up to that limit, choosing a variety of outfits, ranging from casual to dressy to evening wear. There were no dreary or dull colours in her new wardrobe, either. Everything was vibrant and colourful, in keeping with her new blonde hair.

The traffic was bad by the time Emily headed home, peak hour having well and truly arrived. Despite it not being far from the shopping mall at Birkenhead Point to Hunter's Hill, it was rising six by the time she reached home. The sun was very low in the sky and the shadows from the trees around the house were long against the stone walls.

Emily parked her car outside the garage door, then set about the job of carting her parcels up the stairs to her apartment. Once they were all in her bedroom, she spread everything out on her bed, putting the accessories with each outfit.

The dress she was going to wear tonight was exquisite. Made in turquoise silk, it was a wraparound style with a deep V neckline, three-quarter sleeves and a wide matching belt which was heavily beaded. She'd seen the dress displayed in a boutique window and fell in love with it instantly. Fell in love with the accessories as well, which included turquoise sandals and evening bag—also beaded. Completing the outfit were long crystal and turquoise earrings which fell to her shoulders and made her long neck look even longer.

Emily could not wait to put it all on again. But she thought she'd better have a shower first and freshen up her make-up as well. Who knew? Sebastian might make it home by seven, which was less than an hour away.

By twenty to seven she was totally ready and thrilled to bits with her appearance. Her blonde hair looked sensational against the turquoise.

'Now that's a woman who won't look out of place on Sebastian's arm,' she told her reflection.

Not able to sit and wait patiently in her apartment, Emily decided to go over to the main house and wait for Sebastian there. Maybe she could go up to his bedroom and pass the time, working out what kind of furniture and carpet would best suit. Hopefully, she could persuade Sebastian to take tomorrow off work. Then they could get started on ridding the room of Lana's perfume, not to mention her lingering presence.

Sebastian probably hadn't noticed, but there were still some things of Lana's hanging in his wardrobe. Some cosmetics on the vanity unit as well. Plus a half empty bottle of that dreaded perfume.

Emily hadn't dared throw any of it out before this. But tonight, she would.

Taking her evening purse and set of keys with her, Emily had locked her door and turned to walk down the stairs when she noticed a light shining through Sebastian's bedroom window.

He must have just arrived home, she thought excitedly and hurried down the stairs.

'Sebastian!' she called out on entering the downstairs hall.

No answer.

Maybe he'd jumped into the shower and couldn't hear her.

Emily ran up the stairs, thinking how typical it was of a man not to ring her from the airport and let her know he'd managed to get that earlier flight.

Still, perhaps he hadn't wanted to stop, choosing instead to bolt for the taxi rank and jump into the first available taxi.

As she hurried along the upstairs hallway, she couldn't hear any shower running. There again, the walls in this house were extremely solid, unlike modern homes. Hard to hear anything much from room to room.

His bedroom door was slightly ajar. Emily stopped and knocked, calling his name at the same time.

Still no answer.

Emily's chest tightened as she reached out to push the door open. Something was wrong here. Very wrong.

She called Sebastian's name again as she walked in, her stomach contracting the second that hated scent hit her nostrils.

It was too strong. Way too strong.

Lana was lying on the bed, sleeping, wearing nothing but an emerald silk robe. Her riot of red curls were spread out on the pillows, her robe gaping in all the right places.

Clearly, the woman still had keys to Sebastian's home. Also, clearly, she had left her Italian husband and come flying home to Australia, back to her one true love.

Nausea swirled in Emily's stomach, bile rising right up her throat into her mouth. Of all the things she'd imagined happening if she took the risk of becoming involved with Sebastian, this was not one of them. She'd thought—no presumed—Lana was out of their lives for ever.

As though sensing her standing there, Lana woke with a start, then sat up abruptly, her wide green eyes confused as they swept over Emily.

'Who the hell are you?' she demanded to know as she swung her feet over the side of the bed and stood up. 'Oh, don't tell me Sebastian's got himself a new floozy already.'

Emily might have felt sick inside, but no way was she going to show any fear in front of Sebastian's ex-girlfriend.

'Don't you recognise me, Lana?' she said with seeming calm. 'It's Emily.'

'Emily! My goodness, what have you done to yourself? Had an extreme makeover?'

'No. Just had my hair done and bought a few new clothes.'

'Trying to attract Sebastian's attention, no doubt,' Lana sneered, standing up and retying her robe. 'I always knew you were stuck on him. Well you've wasted your time, sweetheart. I'm back and he's still all mine.'

'Not quite,' Emily said and coolly held out her left hand, the diamond sparkling in the lamplight.

Lana stared at her hand, then up at her face. 'Are you telling me you're engaged?'

'Yes.'

'Since when?'

'Since yesterday.'

'My, but you are a fast little worker, aren't you?'

'You've been gone over a month, Lana,' Emily pointed out.

Lana laughed. 'Most of which Seb spent texting me and begging me to come back to him.'

Emily didn't believe that. No way would Sebastian beg anybody for anything.

'In the end he came after me, all the way to Milan.'

'I do know that, Lana,' Emily said coolly. 'He told me. But not to get you back. To have done with you once and for all.'

'Really? I presume then that he didn't tell you that he had sex with me. Less than half an hour before I walked down the aisle. I was wearing my wedding dress at the time, might I add.'

All the blood drained from Emily's face.

'Your fiancé's sexually obsessed with me. Has been ever since the first night we met and I went down on him in the back of a limo. He loves it that I can make him lose control and do things he wouldn't normally do. It drove him crazy, my marrying another man. Which is exactly what I planned. I never intended to stay with that boring, fat old coot. I just wanted to make Seb suffer for not marrying me himself. The way I see it, he only asked you to marry him to punish me. It's a revenge thing. Now that I'm back, he'll drop you like a hot cake. Because I'm the one he really wants. Not you, Miss Ice Cool. You might be able to set a nice dinner table, but I'm the one who lets him screw me on it.'

'In that case, I'll be buying a new dining table as well,' Emily said, determined not to let this creature destroy her. Not to her face, anyway.

'As well as what?' she snapped.

'As well as all the furniture in this room. I don't want any reminders of you hanging around the house.'

Lana laughed. 'Then you'd have to get rid of the whole place. Because I've screwed the master of the house just about everywhere in this place. Even in the garage. I'll bet you'd never let him do you there, Miss Prissy.'

Emily's teeth clenched down hard in her jaw. 'Then you'd be dead wrong, Miss Slut-Face.'

She received some satisfaction from standing up to Lana. But there was no joy for her in this exchange. A great pit was already opening up in her stomach.

'Does Sebastian know you're here?' she asked, not sure what she'd do if this creature said yes.

'No. He does not,' Sebastian snapped.

When Emily whirled to see Sebastian striding into the room, her legs went to jelly. Immediately, Lana ran past her towards him, bursting into crocodile tears at the same time.

'Oh, Seb, I'm so glad you're home,' she sobbed as she threw herself into his arms.

Emily watched, appalled, as Lana snaked her arms up around his neck and pressed her thinly clad body to his.

'I didn't know where else to go,' she cried. 'Alfonso didn't want me. He just married me to hide his homosexuality from his family. He spent our wedding night with his lover.'

What an act, Emily thought disgustedly. And what a story!

* * *

If Sebastian had been a violent man, he would have done violence right at that moment. When he glanced over Lana's shoulder at his lovely Emily, who was looking heart-stoppingly gorgeous, he could see the distress in her eyes. And the disgust.

He hadn't overheard much of their conversation. But he suspected Lana must have said something to upset Emily very much.

With less than gentle movements, he disengaged Lana's talons from the back of his neck and forcibly pushed her away. Then he walked over to put his arm firmly around Emily's waist, drawing her to his side.

'I'm sorry, Lana,' he said coldly, 'but your marital problems are not my concern. You're also not welcome here. In case Emily hasn't told you, we're engaged to be married.'

Lana took a long moment to gather herself, tossing her red curls back from her shoulders as she surveyed the two of them together with calculating green eyes.

'Yes, she told me. Couldn't wait to. But you don't love her, Seb. You love me. You know you do.'

'I know I don't,' he said with a dry laugh. 'I never did. It was just a sexual infatuation, and I'm well and truly over it. And over you.'

'Really? Well, you were still infatuated last week,' she snapped. '*Very* infatuated. Oh, yes, I told little Miss Prissy about what you did.'

'I'm sure you couldn't wait,' he bit out, hating the way Emily stiffened against him. 'Just as I can't wait to get you out of my house.'

Whipping his mobile out of his trouser pocket,

Sebastian flipped it open and ordered a taxi. It didn't take him long to get what he wanted. The taxi company knew he was a very good client.

'There will be a taxi at the kerb outside the gates in ten minutes,' he told a furious-faced Lana. 'Don't keep it waiting.'

'You can't do this to me!' she screamed. 'I'll sue you, you bastard. I'll take you to court for palimony.'

'Do that and you'll lose, *Countess*. The moment you married, you lost all chance of getting a cent out of me. Now, get dressed. Your ten minutes is already ticking away. Come, Emily, the smell in this room is too much for the nose.'

Sebastian steered her from the room, but he could feel the underlying resistance in her body.

'Don't let her ruin things for us, Emily,' he said as he led her along the hallway.

'You had sex with her,' Emily replied, her tone flat and disbelieving. 'In her wedding dress.'

'Look, I didn't go through with it. I stopped once I realised what I was doing. That was why I drank too much on the flight home. Because I was so disgusted with myself for letting that tramp almost seduce me. Trust me when I tell you that I don't love her or want her any more. I'm so over Lana, it isn't funny. You're the one I want, Emily. You have to believe me.'

Emily stopped at the top of the stairs and raised hurt eyes to his.

'No, Sebastian,' she said, her voice hollow and hurt.

'I *don't* have to believe you.' And, loosening her arm from his grip, she ran down the stairs ahead of him.

Sebastian chased after her, full-on panic twisting at his guts. 'What are you going to do?' he called after her.

She didn't reply, just ran faster.

He caught her outside the back door, grabbing her arm and spinning her back to face him. 'You can't run away from me like this. We have to talk this out.'

She shook her head, her face pale but her eyes determined. 'There's nothing to talk about. I can't marry you, Sebastian. Or live in this house with you.'

'But you love this house!'

'I don't any more.'

'Why not? Damn it all, Emily, what did Lana say to you?'

'It doesn't matter.'

'But it does matter. Tell me.'

'Very well. She said you did it everywhere in this house. Even in the garage.'

Sebastian grimaced. Oh, hell.

'I'll buy us a new house,' he said straight away.

She shook her head, her expression sad. 'Oh, Sebastian. You can't buy your way out of this problem. The thing is I...I...'

'You what?'

She shook her head in an anguished fashion. 'I find I can't marry without love after all. It's just not me. I'm sorry, Sebastian. I really am, but I've made up my mind and this time you won't change it. I'll be gone as soon as I can pack all my things. Don't worry about severance pay. I'll waive that in lieu of working out my notice.'

'Don't you dare give me that bloody ring back!' Sebastian snapped when she started easing it off her finger.

'All right,' she returned in that quiet, calm voice which he usually loved but which was driving him mad right now. 'I won't.'

Sebastian frowned, then gaped when she walked over and tossed the ring into the pool. As a gesture went, it was as dramatic as it was awfully final. He watched as she continued to walk away from him with her head held high.

The male ego part of him wanted to race after her and drag her back into his arms.

But the more logical part knew that any caveman technique would not work. Not this time.

So he whirled round and strode back inside to have one final confrontation with Lana before she left. He reached the bottom of the stairs just as she was coming down, bags in hand.

'You knew the Count was gay when you married him, didn't you?' he threw at her.

'Of course,' she snapped.

'He paid you to marry him.'

'My, my, you and Sherlock Holmes would make a good pair. But not you and Miss Prissy. And you know why not, Sebastian? Because she's in love with you.'

'*What?* She told you that, did she?'

'Not in so many words. But I've always known she

was in love with you. Women sense these things about other women. That's why I never could stand her.'

'You're wrong,' he said, thinking that if Emily loved him she wouldn't be leaving him.

Lana laughed. 'What's the problem with her loving you, Sebastian? Not that I don't already know. You don't want a woman's love, do you? Just her body. And, in Emily's case, her ability to run a smooth household. The little fool is going to be miserable, married to you. And you, you cold-blooded bastard, once you get bored with your bland, boring, goody-two-shoes bride, you're going to come looking for me again. And you know what, lover? I won't knock you back. But next time, I'll come at a price.'

'Whores always come at a price, Lana. But I have some news for you. I don't know if Emily loves me or not, but I know *I* love *her*, more than I ever thought possible. Emily is no man's fool. Neither is she bland or boring. She's a warm, intelligent, sexy woman. Oh, yes, *very* sexy, in a way someone like you could never hope to be. Now, get your sorry arse out of here!'

'You're the one who's going to be sorry,' she threatened, her face going bright red.

'Give it a rest, will you?' Sebastian said scornfully as he swept open the front door. 'Go back to Milan, where you can be what you've always been. A vain, shallow poseur.'

Lana huffed and puffed, then stormed out.

Sebastian banged the door shut after her, then turned to walk thoughtfully down to the kitchen.

Could it be possible that Emily loved him?

He hardly dared believe it. For what was there to love about him?

Lana was right. Till recently, he had been a cold-blooded bastard.

Still, he had to find out. Had to make Emily look him in the eyes and tell him that she didn't love him.

CHAPTER FIFTEEN

WHEN the knock came on her door, Emily groaned. She'd been packing as fast as she could, knowing full well that Sebastian would not simply let her leave.

The two suitcases which she'd brought with her eighteen months ago were stuffed full and all the clothes she'd bought today were back in their plastic bags. Another five to ten minutes and she'd have been safely out of here.

Steeling herself for more Sebastian-style arguments, Emily walked to the door and opened it.

'Please don't start again,' she said straight away. 'I'm going shortly and that's final.'

'Do you love me?'

The unexpected question sent all the breath rushing from her lungs.

'Lana said you did,' he went on, his eyes searching hers.

Emily knew that confessing her love for him would be the kiss of death. She'd almost admitted it earlier, stopping herself just in time.

'What would *she* know?' Emily threw back at him.

'That's no answer, Emily. I want to hear you tell me that you don't love me. Because I love you.'

Shock at this even more unexpected statement was swiftly followed by fury.

The crack of her hand slapping his face with all her might echoed through the night air.

Sebastian swore as he lurched back on the small landing, his hand lifting to his reddened cheek, his eyes wide and disbelieving.

'To tell a woman that you love her when you don't is beneath contempt,' Emily cried, tears flooding her eyes. 'Get out!' she yelled, pushing him wildly in the middle of his chest. 'Get out of my sight!'

He grabbed her hands and shook her. 'I'm not lying, Emily. I *do* love you.'

'I don't believe you,' she sobbed. 'I'll never believe you. You're just saying it to get your way.'

'No,' he said, shaking his head. 'I'm not. If you think about it, it's not something I would say if I didn't mean it.'

Emily groaned in despair. Because she knew he would.

'You're upset, Emily, and not thinking straight. Look, Lana's gone. Why don't you come with me over to the house and I'll pour you a brandy? You need to calm down. You're overwrought.'

First lies and now kindness. Next thing he'd start kissing her and she wouldn't know which way was up.

Oh, no, she wasn't falling for that any more!

'I don't want to go over to the house and have a brandy,' she choked out, her shoulders shaking under his grip whilst hot tears cascaded down her face. 'I want to get out of here, away from you.'

Sebastian saw the truth in her face. Heard the truth in her voice. Lana was right. She did love him. For why else would she be like this?

'And I want you to get your hands off me!' she raged on, even as she wept.

Sebastian grimaced as he struggled to do the right thing. His first instinct was to pull her into his arms and show her how much he loved her. But he could see that might backfire on him big time.

'All right,' he muttered, lifting his hands from her shoulders. 'All right. But I don't think you should go anywhere tonight, Emily. You're not in a fit state to drive.'

'Don't you dare tell me what I can and cannot do. I'm an adult woman and I know exactly what I'm capable of. And I know what you're capable of, Sebastian Armstrong! You had sex with her, in her wedding dress!'

Sebastian winced. If only he could go back in time, he'd never have gone to Milan last week. But his ego had driven him on.

Lana had been the first female to break up with him and he simply hadn't been able to handle it. Not because he'd loved her. But because he'd thought of her as his. His pride had been stung by her leaving him for another man.

Emily wasn't leaving him for another man. She was just leaving him. Period.

He had to find a way to handle this better or he was going to lose her. Not just for now, but for forever.

'Where will you go?' he asked quietly.

'That's none of your business.'

Sebastian tried not to panic, reminding himself that she would take her mobile phone with her, no matter where she went. Contacting people was pretty easy these days. If the worst came to the worst, he could hire a private detective to find her.

'This is not the end of us, Emily.'

She dashed the tears from her eyes and gave him a determined look. 'Oh, yes, it is, Sebastian. Now, if you'd please get out of my way, I have a car to pack.'

Sebastian decided offering to help her was not going to work, either. Damn it, but he didn't know what to do. He'd never felt this helpless before. To simply walk away seemed weak and wimpish. But what else could he do?

'I'll be in touch,' he said, before turning and walking slowly back down the stairs, his spirits sinking with each step. His caveman instinct kept warning him that he was making a mistake, letting her go like this. But his sensitive new-age guy side— the one he'd discovered since becoming involved with Emily—told him to be patient.

Good things come to those who wait.

Or so they said.

At the same time, nice guys often did finish last.

If you love someone, you let them go...and they'll come back to you.

He'd read that somewhere.

Sounded like a whole load of bulldust in Sebastian's opinion. But what did he know? He'd never been in love before.

It was sheer hell, this love business.

When he heard Emily's car go down the driveway, it felt as if someone was inside his chest, ripping his heart out. She'd gone. She'd really gone. Lord knew where. She'd said she had no friends.

Suddenly, the house was deathly quiet and depressingly empty.

It was Sebastian who reached for the brandy.

'I'll get her back,' he vowed as he downed the first swallow. 'If not tomorrow, then the next day. Or the next.'

His voice sounded sure. But down deep inside, Sebastian was not convinced.

As she'd said, he could not buy her. Or persuade her with words of love. Because she didn't believe him.

Seducing her a second time wasn't a viable option, either.

Which left what?

For the first time in years, Sebastian was stumped.

CHAPTER SIXTEEN

DR DANIEL BAYLISS was sitting in his lounge room reading, when the front doorbell rang.

With a puzzled glance at his watch, he rose, then went to answer it.

The sight of his estranged daughter standing on his doorstep filled Daniel with instant joy, despite her slightly apprehensive expression. He'd dreamt of this day but never thought it would actually happen.

'Emily!' he exclaimed. 'How lovely to see you. Come in. Come in.'

'Oh, Daddy,' she cried, her face suddenly crumpling.

Daniel's heart lurched. His daughter hadn't called him Daddy since she was about ten years old.

He did what any father would do. He gathered her into his arms and just hugged her, tears filling his own eyes. Now he knew how the father of the prodigal son had felt. Only this time it was more the case of the prodigal father.

Had Emily forgiven him at last for what he'd done?

He sure hoped so.

But he suspected it wasn't forgiveness which had brought his daughter home to him. It was something else.

'Come inside,' he said gently at last and led her down to the kitchen, sitting her at the large country-style table whilst he popped on the kettle, then took the box of tissues which he kept on the counter and placed them next to her.

He didn't say anything. Or ask anything. He just stood there and waited till Emily was ready to talk.

'You're looking well,' she said at last.

'You are too.' Better than she'd ever looked.

She laughed, then sobbed, her eyes filling anew. He moved forward and held the tissue box out to her. She snatched several out and shook her head, clearly annoyed with herself for crying again.

'Where's Barbra?' she asked after she'd blown her nose and gathered herself.

'In Africa, working for the United Nations.'

Emily frowned. 'You didn't marry her?'

'No. I realised after you left that I didn't love her. Whether you believe me or not, your mother was the only woman I have ever really loved.'

'Then why were you unfaithful to her?'

Daniel shook his head. 'A lot of men are unfaithful to wives they love, Emily. Sometimes it's difficult to explain why. Sex to a man is not always an expression of love. Sometimes it caters for an entirely different need. With some men, the need is just sexual. Or perhaps the craving for a new experience.

Some excitement to spice up their mundane lives. With me, I think it was the need to know I was still alive. And, of course, my ego was flattered by Barbra's attentions. I'm sorry that you found out I wasn't the hero you always imagined me to be, Emily. But the awful truth is that most men aren't heroes. They're just human beings, with all the faults and flaws that go with being a male.'

'You're right there,' she said with the kind of bitterness which only came from a personal and very recent hurt.

Daniel realised things had to be very bad indeed to send his daughter running home to him. When she'd left eighteen months ago she'd said she would never talk to him again as long as she lived.

And he'd believed her.

Emily was a deceptive character, her seemingly calm, compassionate personality hiding a heart that could be as wildly emotional as it could be incredibly stubborn. A typical Scorpio, once wronged, she found it very hard to forgive.

'Why don't you tell me about him?' he asked gently.

Her eyes flashed up to his.

'Come now,' he said. 'This is why you came home, isn't it? To have a loving shoulder to cry on. And I do love you, Emily. I'm your father. I've also been known to give a few words of wisdom in my day. Doctoring isn't always about prescribing pills, you know. The best medicine is often a sympathetic ear and some sensible suggestions.'

'As long as you don't tell me I've been a fool.'

'Why? Have you been?'

She nodded. 'Yes. A big fool.'

'Then I don't need to tell you that, do I? Now, let me get us both a nice cup of tea, and then you can tell me all about what you've been up to this past eighteen months.'

Emily told him everything.

It wasn't easy, especially when it came to relating what had happened during the last few days. But she didn't leave anything out. What was the point in confiding, if you left things out?

He didn't interrupt. Or ask stupid questions. He just let her talk. And talk. Then talk some more.

Finally, she related the argument she'd had with Sebastian tonight, plus her dramatic exit.

'I should never have agreed to marry him in the first place,' she said wretchedly. 'But I was weak. At first, I just wanted to go to bed with him. And then…then I wanted to stay there.'

Daniel sighed. 'Sexual desire can be a very powerful drive, Emily.'

'That's why I had to get away,' she cried. 'If I'd stayed, he might have tried to get me back into bed. And I probably would have gone. I just can't think straight when I'm around him.'

'You love him.'

'Maybe I don't. Maybe it's just what you felt for Barbra.'

'You don't believe that, Emily. And neither do I.

I know you. You love this man. And he loves you, if I'm not badly mistaken.'

Emily stared at her father across the kitchen table. 'How can you say that?'

'Emily, no man proposes marriage to their house-keeper just to stop her from leaving, no matter how good she is at her job.'

Emily shook her head. 'You don't understand. Sebastian does things differently from most men. He doesn't follow conventional standards. Trust me when I say he doesn't love me. What he loves is a peaceful, well run home, with no hassles. I created that for him. That's why he proposed. To keep the status quo. If he got a convenient bed-partner thrown into the bargain, then so much the better.'

'Maybe that was true, to begin with,' her father conceded. 'But something changed along the line, probably down in that hotel in Wollongong. Because that didn't sound like a very peaceful episode you had with him earlier tonight. Hell, girl, you called him a liar, screamed at him and slapped his face. Yet he still wants you. Trust *me*. That's love.'

Emily opened her mouth, then closed it again. 'You really think so?'

'I really think so,' her father replied firmly. 'So yes, Emily, you have been a fool. But not in the way you think. You started being a fool the moment you walked away without doing what your Sebastian asked you to do. Calm down and talk things over.'

'But he...he had sex with that disgusting woman! Less than a week ago!'

'So what.'

'*So what?*'

'Yes, so what. Clearly, he was disgusted with himself afterwards. Tell me, daughter, did he stand by you when that woman showed up?'

'Yes…'

'Did he look at her like he wanted to screw her right then and there?'

'No…'

'Did he show her the door in no uncertain terms?'

'Yes, but…'

'But nothing. The man deserves a medal for exemplary conduct under difficult conditions. And what did you do? You threw his ring into a swimming pool.'

'Well, I…I…'

'Look, do you or do you not love this man?'

'I've just spent the last hour telling you that I do!'

'Good. Now, I have one other thing to clear up in your female mind. You said he made love to you in the garage yesterday, is that right?'

Emily flushed at the memory of their hot encounter against his car. 'Yes. And he made love to *her* in the garage too!'

'No, he didn't. He had sex with her in the garage. You, he made love to. How old did you say Sebastian was?'

'Forty.'

'Forty,' her father repeated drily. 'For heaven's sake, Emily, a man of his age and wealth will have had any number of women. I doubt this Lana is the first female he's had in a garage. Or on a stupid dining table. One of the reasons you fell in love with him in the first place is because he's an experienced man of the world. I know you, Emily. You like successful men. You like it that they know what meal to order and what wine to drink. *And* how to make love properly. Even when you were a teenager your boyfriends were always several years older than you. They all dressed well and drove flashy cars.'

Emily had to agree. 'Yes, they did, didn't they?'

'You will enjoy being the wife of a billionaire. Especially one who loves you.'

'You really think he does?'

'I do. But what I think doesn't matter. What do *you* think?'

'I think I would be very foolish to believe that without further evidence. But I also think I should go back and find out for myself.'

'What a sensible girl.'

'Besides, something else has just occurred to me.'

'What?'

'When we did it in the garage yesterday, we…um…didn't use any protection.'

Her father frowned. 'You mean you might be pregnant?'

'It's possible.'

'Then you very definitely need to go back and talk to him.'

'What time is it?'

'Only just after ten-thirty. Hunter's Hill is no more than a twenty-minute drive at this time of night. Why don't you go back before you can find another reason why you shouldn't?'

Emily grimaced. 'The moment I show up, he's going to think he's won.'

'Somehow I doubt that. You have no idea how formidable you can be, Emily, when you really lose your temper.'

She sighed, then rose to her feet. 'Maybe he won't want me any more. I did hit him. Once. Then pushed him. And he hates that kind of thing.'

'He'll still want you. I'd put my money on it. Now, off you go.'

She smiled. 'Thank you, Dad. I do love you too, you know. I always have.'

'You've no idea how relieved I am to hear that, Emily,' he said with a catch in his voice. 'I've missed you terribly.'

She drew back and looked deep into his eyes, only then realising how much their estrangement had hurt him. She'd been trying to punish him, of course. But enough was enough.

'It was wrong of me to cut you out of my life like that,' she said with true regret.

'I was the one who was wrong. I can't tell you how glad I am that your mother never knew. She...she didn't, did she?'

'No.'

'Thank God.'

'Now, get along with you. And listen to what the man has to say this time. Really listen and don't judge.'

'I will, Dad. Look, I probably won't be back tonight,' she added quickly. 'But I'll call you tomorrow. I promise.'

CHAPTER SEVENTEEN

'MUSTN'T call her mobile number yet,' Sebastian muttered into his brandy balloon as the grandfather clock in the hallway chimed eleven. 'Must be patient.'

Damn, but that was a noisy clock when there was no one else in the house.

'You know what they say about people who drink alone.'

Sebastian shot to his feet at the sound of Emily's voice, the brandy swirling in the bottom of the glass as he spun round.

She was standing in the double doorway which led out into the hallway, something in her eyes preventing him from hoping this was going to be an instantly happy reunion.

'I didn't hear you drive up,' he said, sitting back down in the armchair again with a sigh.

'The clock was chiming.'

'Aah…'

'I've calmed down.'

She looked *too* calm in his opinion. But very

beautiful. He loved her new hair. And that gorgeous blue dress. What he would not give to have taken her to dinner tonight and had a lovely romantic evening. Instead, he'd had to contend with Lana showing up and his life being turned upside down.

'I've come back to talk,' she said. 'Like you suggested.'

All of a sudden, he no longer wanted to talk to her. Which was perverse. Maybe it was all the brandy he'd drunk. Or maybe it was that wariness in her eyes.

Whatever, he just wanted to go back into his cave.

'I think I've said all I have to say, Emily,' he told her in a weary voice, then took another sip of brandy. 'I can't make you believe that I love you.'

'Just tell me when? *When* did you decide you loved me?'

'When?'

'Yes, when?'

Women! Why did they have to scrutinise and analyse everything? Why couldn't she just accept his word for it? It would be so much easier.

'Tonight.'

'When tonight? When you found you needed a reason to stop me from leaving?'

Sebastian shot her a frustrated look. 'You really do have trust issues where men are concerned, don't you? It was when I walked into my bedroom and saw the distress in your eyes. I took one look at that bitch, Lana, and I wanted to kill her with my bare hands. Which is so not me it isn't funny. I despise violence of any kind. But when a man loves a woman, his protective instinct becomes very fierce. Or so I've gathered.'

'What do you mean, so you've gathered?'

Sebastian shrugged. 'I thought falling in love wasn't something I was capable of. I've never fallen in love before.'

'If you didn't love Lana, then why did you run after her and have sex with her?'

'My stupid male ego ran after her. And my stupid male body had sex with her. For a few seconds, Emily. That's all. Once I realised what I was doing, and what kind of creature I was doing it with, I stopped. Afterwards, I couldn't get away from her fast enough, or back to Australia fast enough. That's why I caught an earlier flight. Because all I wanted was to get home to you. When I read your resignation letter, Emily, I felt a million times worse than when Lana left me. Her, I could do without. But not you, Emily. I discovered I could not do without you.'

No one could doubt the bleakness in his eyes or the sincerity of his words. Maybe her father was right. Maybe he did love her after all.

'*Why* did you think you weren't capable of falling in love?' Emily asked.

He looked hard at her, his eyes grim. 'You really want to know?'

'Yes, of course.' Why did he think she'd come back, if not to understand him?

'Your father was unfaithful to your mother,' he said. 'My father *murdered* my mother.'

'*What?*' Emily exclaimed, feeling both shocked and bewildered. 'I thought you said your parents died in a car accident.'

'It was put down as a car accident. But it was murder. I was in the car. I *know* what happened.'

Emily shook her head in absolute horror.

'They were arguing at the time,' Sebastian went on, his voice tight with contained emotion. 'They always argued when they didn't have any money to buy pot. When drug addicts are off the weed, they have an anger management problem. Usually, their anger was directed at me. This time, however, I was out of reach, huddled in the back seat of the car. Anyway, Mum said something to Dad about his being a loser and a dole bludger and he went berserk. Called her every name in the book. Told her she was a useless f— mother who couldn't even look after one miserable kid. Which was true. I used to go to school without any lunch and dressed in dirty clothes.'

Emily grimaced, nausea swirling in her stomach. What kind of mother treated her child like that?

Sebastian's eyes reflected the effort it was taking for him to tell her the truth. 'Finally, Dad said he'd show her who the loser in this family was and he drove the car straight at a telegraph pole. Mum was killed outright. Dad died in hospital a few days later. I got out without a scratch.'

Oh, no, you didn't, Emily thought, her heart contracting as she stared into his suddenly dead eyes. You were left with lots of scratches. Inside.

But it explained so much about this man she loved. His need to succeed. His love of nice things. Even his asking her to marry him—a woman he believed was calm and capable. Nothing like his own neglectful and abusive mother.

'And then you went to live with your grand-mother,' she said gently.

'What? Yes. Yes, that's right.'

'Oh, Sebastian, I'm so sorry.'

'For what?'

'For everything. No child should have to go through something like that.'

'No,' he agreed. 'And no child of mine will. Not that I'll have children now.'

'What do you mean?'

'I have no intention of having children outside of marriage. And the only woman I've ever loved won't marry me. You threw my ring in the pool.'

'What if I'm already pregnant?'

He blinked at her. 'How? Oh, you mean that episode in the garage yesterday. You'd have to be very unlucky to conceive on that one occasion.'

'Or lucky,' she said. 'Depending on how you look at it.'

His eyes narrowed, his fingers tightening around the brandy balloon. 'And how would you look at it, Emily?'

She crossed the room to kneel down on the carpet by his feet, resting her hands and face against his knees. 'I would love to have your child, Sebastian,' she said softly. 'I *do* believe you love me. And I really want to marry you.'

Sebastian's hand shook as he put down his brandy, then tipped her chin up with his fingertips. 'You really mean that? You're not just saying it because you might be pregnant?'

'I would never just say something like that, Sebastian. I love you very much. I've loved you for quite some time.'

His eyes shimmered as they searched hers. 'How long is quite some time?'

'I realised my true feelings after Lana left you. But I didn't think I had a chance with you, so I decided to leave.'

'Why didn't you just say yes straight away when I proposed?'

'Because I wanted you to love me, not just marry me.'

'Then why did you throw my ring in the pool tonight after I *told* you I loved you?'

'Because I'm a fool.'

Sebastian groaned as he reached down and lifted her up into his lap. He didn't kiss her, just held her tight, his lips in her hair.

'You made me almost despair tonight,' he confessed huskily.

Emily was struggling not to weep. 'I'm sorry,' she choked out.

'Don't ever leave me again.'

'I won't.'

'I'll sell this house if it makes you unhappy.'

Emily pulled back and shook her head. 'No. You were right, I love this house. We'll just redo the master bedroom. Oh, and replace the dining table.'

'The dining table! What's wrong with the dining table?'

Emily bit her bottom lip. 'Um…Lana said you had sex with her on it.'

'I what? That's a bald-faced lie!'

'You didn't?'

'Never!' Sebastian denied heatedly.

Emily smiled up at him. 'I'm so glad. I really like that table. Now, there's something I have to go and get,' she said as she scrambled off his lap. 'Something I left behind.'

'What?'

'Stay here,' she commanded. 'Don't move. I won't be more than ten seconds.'

She was gone a full minute. Sebastian was about to get up and follow her when he heard a noise behind him. He turned and she was standing there, naked and dripping wet.

'My God, Emily,' he gasped, lurching to his feet.

'I had to get my ring,' she explained as she came forward. 'I knew you'd have left it in the pool.'

He smiled as he pulled her shivering body into his arms. 'Well, it wasn't much good to me without you.'

His hands moved up and down her back, his lower

body hard up against hers, his instant arousal pressing into the soft swell of her stomach.

'I think it's time we continued with our baby-making project,' he said, scooping her up into his arms and carrying her, not towards the stairs but out to the pool. 'How's the water?' he asked as he lowered her to her feet, then began stripping.

'Lovely and warm, once you're in.'

They jumped in together at the deep end, kissing under the water before they surfaced.

'What do you think would have happened if you'd let me join you in here last Friday night?' Sebastian asked as she wound her arms around his neck and her legs around his hips.

'I don't know,' Emily replied. 'What do *you* think would have happened?'

'This,' he growled.

Emily gasped as Sebastian entered her.

'Then this,' he added, cupping her buttocks with his hands and beginning to move her back and forth against him.

Her lips parted on a sigh, her eyes growing heavy with pleasure.

'Tell me you love me,' he commanded.

'I love you,' she said and smiled at him.

He smiled back. 'You were so right, my darling. Sex *with* love is much better than without. We're going to be so happy, you and I. And we're going to be the best parents in the whole wide world.'

* * *

They married beside the pool two months later, their first child—a daughter—arriving seven months after the happy event. They called her Amanda, which meant 'worthy to be loved'.

Emily's father never remarried. He became a close friend of Sebastian's, a devoted grandfather and an even better doctor.

0307 Gen Std HB

MILLS & BOON®

Live the emotion

APRIL 2007 HARDBACK TITLES

ROMANCE™

The Ruthless Marriage Proposal *Miranda Lee* 978 0 263 19604 7
Bought for the Greek's Bed *Julia James* 978 0 263 19605 4
The Greek Tycoon's Virgin Mistress *Chantelle Shaw*
978 0 263 19606 1
The Sicilian's Red-Hot Revenge *Kate Walker* 978 0 263 19607 8
The Italian Prince's Pregnant Bride *Sandra Marton*
978 0 263 19608 5
Kept by the Spanish Billionaire *Cathy Williams* 978 0 263 19609 2
The Kristallis Baby *Natalie Rivers* 978 0 263 19610 8
Mediterranean Boss, Convenient Mistress *Kathryn Ross*
978 0 263 19611 5
A Mother for the Tycoon's Child *Patricia Thayer*
978 0 263 19612 2
The Boss and His Secretary *Jessica Steele* 978 0 263 19613 9
Billionaire on her Doorstep *Ally Blake* 978 0 263 19614 6
Married by Morning *Shirley Jump* 978 0 263 19615 3
Princess Australia *Nicola Marsh* 978 0 263 19616 0
The Sheikh's Contract Bride *Teresa Southwick* 978 0 263 19617 7
The Surgeon and the Single Mum *Lucy Clark* 978 0 263 19618 4
The Surgeon's Longed-For Bride *Emily Forbes* 978 0 263 19619 1

HISTORICAL ROMANCE™

A Scoundrel of Consequence *Helen Dickson* 978 0 263 19757 0
An Innocent Courtesan *Elizabeth Beacon* 978 0 263 19758 7
The King's Champion *Catherine March* 978 0 263 19759 4

MEDICAL ROMANCE™

Single Father, Wife Needed *Sarah Morgan* 978 0 263 19796 9
The Italian Doctor's Perfect Family *Alison Roberts*
978 0 263 19797 6
A Baby of Their Own *Gill Sanderson* 978 0 263 19798 3
His Very Special Nurse *Margaret McDonagh*
978 0 263 19799 0

MILLS & BOON®

0307 Gen Std LP

Live the emotion

APRIL 2007 LARGE PRINT TITLES

ROMANCE™

The Christmas Bride *Penny Jordan*   978 0 263 19439 6
Reluctant Mistress, Blackmailed Wife *Lynne Graham*
    978 0 263 19440 X
At the Greek Tycoon's Pleasure *Cathy Williams* 978 0 263 19441 8
The Virgin's Price *Melanie Milburne*   978 0 263 19442 6
The Bride of Montefalco *Rebecca Winters*   978 0 263 19443 4
Crazy about the Boss *Teresa Southwick*   978 0 263 19444 2
Claiming the Cattleman's Heart *Barbara Hannay*
    978 0 263 19445 0
Blind-Date Marriage *Fiona Harper*   978 0 263 19446 9

HISTORICAL ROMANCE™

An Improper Companion *Anne Herries*   978 0 263 19388 8
The Viscount *Lyn Stone*   978 0 263 19389 6
The Vagabond Duchess *Claire Thornton*   978 0 263 19390 X

MEDICAL ROMANCE™

Rescue at Cradle Lake *Marion Lennox*   978 0 263 19343 8
A Night to Remember *Jennifer Taylor*   978 0 263 19344 6
The Doctors' New-Found Family *Laura MacDonald*
    978 0 263 19345 4
Her Very Special Consultant *Joanna Neil*   978 0 263 19346 2
A Surgeon, A Midwife: A Family *Gill Sanderson* 978 0 263 19537 6
The Italian Doctor's Bride *Margaret McDonagh* 978 0 263 19538 4

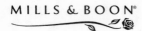

MILLS & BOON®

MAY 2007 HARDBACK TITLES

ROMANCE™

Bought: The Greek's Bride *Lucy Monroe*   978 0 263 19620 7
The Spaniard's Blackmailed Bride *Trish Morey*
978 0 263 19621 4
Claiming His Pregnant Wife *Kim Lawrence*   978 0 263 19622 1
Contracted: A Wife for the Bedroom *Carol Marinelli*
978 0 263 19623 8
Willingly Bedded, Forcibly Wedded *Melanie Milburne*
978 0 263 19624 5
Count Giovanni's Virgin *Christina Hollis*   978 0 263 19625 2
The Millionaire Boss's Baby *Maggie Cox*   978 0 263 19626 9
The Italian's Defiant Mistress *India Grey*   978 0 263 19627 6
The Forbidden Brother *Barbara McMahon*   978 0 263 19628 3
The Lazaridis Marriage *Rebecca Winters*   978 0 263 19629 0
Bride of the Emerald Isle *Trish Wylie*   978 0 263 19630 6
Her Outback Knight *Melissa James*   978 0 263 19631 3
The Cowboy's Secret Son *Judy Christenberry* 978 0 263 19632 0
Best Friend...Future Wife *Claire Baxter*   978 0 263 19633 7
A Father for Her Son *Rebecca Lang*   978 0 263 19634 4
The Surgeon's Marriage Proposal *Molly Evans*   978 0 263 19635 1

HISTORICAL ROMANCE™

Dishonour and Desire *Juliet Landon*   978 0 263 19760 0
An Unladylike Offer *Christine Merrill*   978 0 263 19761 7
The Roman's Virgin Mistress *Michelle Styles*   978 0 263 19762 4

MEDICAL ROMANCE™

Single Dad, Outback Wife *Amy Andrews*   978 0 263 19800 3
A Wedding in the Village *Abigail Gordon*   978 0 263 19801 0
In His Angel's Arms *Lynne Marshall*   978 0 263 19802 7
The French Doctor's Midwife Bride *Fiona Lowe*
978 0 263 19803 4

MAY 2007 LARGE PRINT TITLES

ROMANCE™

The Italian's Future Bride *Michelle Reid*	978 0 263 19447 0
Pleasured in the Billionaire's Bed *Miranda Lee*	
	978 0 263 19448 7
Blackmailed by Diamonds, Bound by Marriage *Sarah Morgan*	
	978 0 263 19449 4
The Greek Boss's Bride *Chantelle Shaw*	978 0 263 19450 0
Outback Man Seeks Wife *Margaret Way*	978 0 263 19451 7
The Nanny and the Sheikh *Barbara McMahon*	978 0 263 19452 4
The Businessman's Bride *Jackie Braun*	978 0 263 19453 1
Meant-To-Be Mother *Ally Blake*	978 0 263 19454 8

HISTORICAL ROMANCE™

Not Quite a Lady *Louise Allen*	978 0 263 19391 6
The Defiant Debutante *Helen Dickson*	978 0 263 19392 3
A Noble Captive *Michelle Styles*	978 0 263 19393 0

MEDICAL ROMANCE™

The Christmas Marriage Rescue *Sarah Morgan*	978 0 263 19347 3
Their Christmas Dream Come True *Kate Hardy*	
	978 0 263 19348 0
A Mother in the Making *Emily Forbes*	978 0 263 19349 7
The Doctor's Christmas Proposal *Laura Iding*	978 0 263 19350 3
Her Miracle Baby *Fiona Lowe*	978 0 263 19539 2
The Doctor's Longed-for Bride *Judy Campbell*	978 0 263 19540 8